Double-Dealing
at Dirtville

Abe Gibson reckoned Dirtville to be as good a place as any in which to live a peaceable life. He had good friends, his saloon was doing well and the town had law. Then, within the space of a few days, everything changed.

It had all started when Zach Holmes, the town telegrapher, had to relay a couple of strange messages to the sheriff. Shortly afterwards the stranger Ethan Grant was gunned down at one of Abe's card tables. Then a beautiful woman shot herself in the head beside Grant's grave.

As all hell broke loose, Abe figured that there had to be one person behind it all. But could he solve the mystery?

Double-Dealing at Dirtville

CLAY MORE

A Black Horse Western

ROBERT HALE · LONDON

ISBN 0 7090 7816 1

Robert Hale Limited
Clerkenwell House
Clerkenwell Green
London EC1R 0HT

*In memory of my grandfather,
who actually saw Buffalo Bill Cody
and who taught me how to tell a yarn.*

Typeset by
Derek Doyle & Associates, Shaw Heath.
Printed and bound in Great Britain by
Antony Rowe Limited, Wiltshire

PROLOGUE

Walt Burnett was madder than a coyote that had been done out of his dinner by a thieving buzzard. His weather-beaten face was redder than usual as he urged his big black up the saguaro and cardon cactus-lined trail from the Rocking WB spread to the Pintos foothills.

When he eventually crested the rise and looked down into the mine camp he scowled. Work had stopped and the two men were sitting by a fire sipping coffee from battered old tin cups and smoking. Water trickling down through the series of rocker cradles was the only evidence of mining activity. Even the mule tied up to the *arrastra* rock-crushing machine was standing still, munching greedily on feed in its nosebag, while the two men laughed and joked.

Burnett rode into the camp and immediately started berating the younger of the two men. He reached into his vest and held out a paper in a fist that trembled with rage. The younger man stood and watched contemptuously as the rancher let out a tirade of invective. The third man hung his head when the rancher suddenly turned his ire on him. Then the younger man began to argue back. From a pocket he held out a bag, opened it and poured glittering dust into the palm of his hand.

Burnett eyed him for moments, then his anger peaked. He stepped forward and dashed the bag from his hand. Then his hand shot out, lashing the other hard across the face. And with a final curse he turned and made for his horse.

He had the reins in his left hand and his right on the pommel of the saddle, ready to put foot in stirrup when the knife thudded into his back, penetrating his heart and propelling him forward against the black's side. He fell dying as the horse panicked and dashed forward.

The young man turned as the third man started to yell at him. Then the gun at his side cleared leather and two bullets hammered into the man's chest, throwing him back to land on the fire.

As he pulled the knife from Walt Burnett's dead body the young man grinned, unaware of the pair of eyes that had watched in horror from the top of the rise.

ONE

Abe Gibson was not a religious man. He'd never found much need for the Good Book or the preachers who peddled its message, then told you how mean and wicked you were, usually just before they stuck a collecting-box in your ribs and robbed you of good drinking-money. For nigh on half a century he had made his way in the south-west, done most things that weren't downright illegal and eventually accumulated enough *dinero* to buy the once down-at-heel drinking-hole that passed as one of Dirtville's three saloons. In the five years he had run it, business had thrived and it had become Dirtville's premier saloon.

He was feeling pretty content with himself that morning after breakfast, especially since he had caught that itinerant preacher cheating at the poker-table the night before and personally ejected him from the saloon with a couple of well-placed kicks. 'No sir,' he mused as he sat on the canopied boardwalk in front of the Dead Ringer saloon, enjoying his first cigar of the day and his second coffee. 'In a perfect world there ain't no need for religion, or preachers.'

'You need preachers to plant them poor bastards,' returned Zach Holmes, the local telegrapher, who sat beside him sipping his second coffee laced with whiskey.

'Who?'

'Them!' replied Zach, pointing the stem of his well-chewed pipe at the cemetery on the hill. 'We all end up on Boot Hill one day. You and me both will be wanting a preacher some day, Abe. Be an idea if'n you didn't aggrieve too many of them.'

The two men were still guffawing at the joke when a buzzer sounded through the open door of the telegraph office next door to the saloon.

'Damn and blast,' Zach cursed, springing to his feet at the sound and heading for the door to take the incoming message. 'This place is getting to be too damned busy for my liking. Too many business moguls and too many folks with nothing else to do but send damn fool messages all day long.'

Abe sucked on his cigar and grinned at his friend's discomfiture. He vaguely listened to the tick-tacking noise of the telegraph sounder as Zach took the incoming message, all the time wondering at the magic of the telegraph system that enabled even small south-western towns like Dirtville to receive information at the press of a key.

A few moments later Zach Holmes came dashing out of the office, his green telegrapher's visor pushed back on his bald dome, a telegram clutched in his hand.

'More for the business mogul?' the saloon-keeper asked with a mischievous grin, for a goodly proportion of the telegrams that arrived in Dirtville were for the attention of Grover Wilkins.

Zach shook his head seriously. 'Law business again. Second telegram in as many days. Sounds serious.'

Abe said no more, but merely watched as the telegrapher put a couple of fingers to his mouth and let out a high-pitched whistle, which resulted in the appearance of a ragged group of street urchins from a nearby alleyway. He singled out a dirty-faced lad of about twelve and handed him the telegram and a couple of coins.

'OK, vamoose,' Zach said. 'This one's for the sheriff, straight away.'

Immediately Vamoose scuttled across the street followed by his gang of equally ragged fellows in the direction of the sheriff's office. Zach sat down again.

'Poor kids,' he said. 'The town ought to do something more for them. It ain't right just letting them wander about without folks to look after them, scratching a living however they can.'

Abe nodded agreement. Street urchins were a constant reminder that so much was wrong with society all the way across the south-west. He knew it was a sore point with Zach. He loosened the cork in the bottle of whiskey under his chair and poured a shot into Zach's cooling coffee.

He was curious about the telegram to the sheriff.

Sheriff Mat Hughes looked down at the two telegraph messages that lay side by side on his desk. He ran the back of his hand against the stubble on his chin and pursed his lips thoughtfully. He was puzzled.

He picked up the first telegraph slip, which had arrived the evening before. It was a simple unsigned message that said simply:

THE THIEF IS ON HIS WAY. ARREST AND DETAIN HIM.

He screwed it up and reaching over, shoved it in the front of the pot-bellied stove. Then he picked the other up. It was from the constable of Hagsworth, the nearest town, a full day's ride away. He read it through again, then casually struck a light to the quirly he had built before Vamoose the urchin had brought him the telegram.

'Is it trouble, Sheriff?' Burt Lister, the young deputy, asked from the other side of the desk. There was a hint of excitement in his voice at the prospect.

Sheriff Hughes nodded as he let a stream of smoke escape from between his thin lips.

'Could be, Burt,' he said. 'Listen up. It's from Constable Veach over at Hagsworth.' And he read the telegram verbatim:

'To Sheriff Mat Hughes, be on the lookout for Ethan Grant, dangerous thief and murderer, believed to be heading to Dirtville. Murdered two men sometime yesterday afternoon. Walt Burnett, owner of Rocking WB Ranch by stab in the back, and Hank Turner, a miner, with a couple of shots in the chest. Stole two bags of gold-dust. Description – age mid-twenties, six feet tall, wears John B Stetson with

snakeskin band, elk-hide vest and ivory-handled Navy Colt. Probably riding a pinto with Rocking WB brand, and Texas rig. Arrest and detain. Extreme caution advised. George Veech.'

Burt Lister smacked his thigh. 'A bit of excitement, huh, Sheriff.' And as he spoke he drew out his Remington .45 and spun the cylinder, inspecting the loaded six chambers. 'You figure he'll come this way?'

Mat Hughes stood up and ground his cigarette stub out on the floor.

'I reckon so. But listen up, Burt, this *hombre* sounds like poison. Neither of us will take any chances.'

The youth grinned, his eyes cold and humourless, like a reptile's.

'Don't you worry none, Sheriff. I ain't going to take any chances with no killer.' He holstered his well-oiled weapon. 'Just as long as he doesn't take any chances with me.'

Evening shadows were falling when the man on the pinto cantered into Dirtville. He made his way directly to the Dead Ringer saloon, dismounted and hitched his mount on the rail, before pushing open the batwing doors.

A fair crowd had already gathered in the saloon; cliques of drinkers clustered along the length of the bar, quaffing beer or sipping whiskey as they bantered about their individual day's business, while others settled down at one of the four gaming-tables in an attempt to win money from their compatriots or, even better, from the house. A thin haze of

11

tobacco smoke had already begun to form and was threatening the singing voices of the three Clover Belles, the Dead Ringer's temporary song and dance show. Abe Gibson had already wondered at how long the girls would stay, on account of the absence of the piano-player that he had promised them when he signed them up.

The stranger walked to the bar and was greeted affably by Abe Gibson himself, an inevitable cigar clamped between his teeth. He liked to tend bar for an hour or so in the evenings when Nathaniel, his head barkeep took his meal. 'You look thirsty, mister,' he said. 'Need to wet your whistle? We got just about all a man could need here.'

The stranger took off his John B Stetson with the snakeskin band and wiped his forehead. He grinned at the singing trio.

'Everything, huh?'

Abe's smile dropped. 'I meant everything a man could want to drink,' he said coldly. 'The Clover Belles are good girls and you're welcome to listen and ogle some, but no one touches them. This ain't no cathouse, savvy!'

The newcomer replaced his hat and stared Abe straight in the eyes, his grin having similarly vanished. Then he adjusted his gunbelt a fraction, a motion that Abe Gibson was cognizant of, and his own hand dropped below the bar to the sawn-off shotgun that he kept poised in readiness on a couple of nails. But the man grinned and nodded his head.

'I understand what you're saying, mister. I didn't mean anything disrespectful. I was just admiring the beautiful women you have here in Dirtville. Just gimme a bottle of your best tonsil paint and direct me to a game and I'll be happy and no trouble to anyone.'

Abe served the man with a good humour that belied his real feelings. There was something about the man that he didn't care too much for. Part of that feeling, he was aware, stemmed from the chat he had had with Zach Holmes that morning, right after he had delivered the telegram to the sheriff.

An hour went by and the stranger became ever more voluble. Abe saw that he had joined a stud-poker game, and had lost more than a little *dinero* to Flash Dan Brady, one of the professional gamblers who plied his profession in the Dirtville drinking-dens.

'Looks like you're out of coin now, friend,' said Flash Dan in a voice deliberately raised so that Abe could hear, in case there was trouble.

'I'm good for ten times the money we've played for,' returned the stranger, his voice slightly slurred from the half-bottle of whiskey he had consumed.

'Need to show it, not talk it,' said Flash Dan.

There were four other players seated round the table. Two of them, sensing possible trouble, made excuses and cashed in their hands.

Abe moved closer towards the table.

'Problem, gents?' he asked.

'No problem,' replied the man with the snakeskin hatband. He reached inside his elk-hide vest and drew out a small sack. He pulled open its purse-string and with a grin let a trickle of gold-dust cascade into his free hand. 'I figure you'd have to go a long way to see gold of this grade.'

Flash Dan's eyes gleamed with interest. He sipped a beer and nodded.

'I reckon we can continue, as long as we agree how much that dust is worth.' He looked up at Abe. 'You able to weigh this out and give us a price, Mr Gibson?' he asked.

Abe nodded to one of his employees. The man disappeared into a back office and reappeared a few moments later with a set of assay scales. In the time that he had been gone, news of the bag of gold-dust had spread around the saloon like wildfire and people stopped talking, turning their attention instead to the events taking place at the stud-poker table. Even the husky Clover Belles went silent.

As the weighing proceeded at the table the stranger downed another glass of whiskey, wiped his mouth with the back of his hand and leaned back contentedly.

'Reckon I'm gonna win all my money back soon,' he jibed, seemingly savouring the attention that was being directed at him. 'As long as the cards come off the top of the deck,' he added unpleasantly.

The gambler's eyes flashed up at him and he stiffened in his chair.

'Are you implying that I'm cheating you?' he demanded through clenched teeth.

'He isn't implying anything!' came a sudden harsh voice. And with a couple of firm paces Sheriff Mat Hughes was standing over the table appraising the stranger. 'I'm the sheriff of Dirtville,' he announced, touching his star with a thumb. 'We ain't used to people flashing bags of golddust around Dirtville. Mind telling me where you got it from?'

'That's my damned business!' the other snapped, visibly tensing.

'What's your name, pilgrim?' Sheriff Hughes asked, his demeanour stern and rigid.

'Again, that's none of your business.'

'That so? Well, maybe it is. You see,' Hughes said, pulling out the telegram that he had received that morning, 'this here is what you might call a warrant for a man's arrest. A man riding a pinto horse with a Texas rig.' His eyes looked up for a moment, registering the beads of perspiration that had suddenly accumulated on the other's upper lip. 'And what did I see on my way in here, but a saddled-up pinto. Oh yeah, and there is a description of a man in his twenties, wearing a John B Stetson with a snakeskin band. Can't be too many of those round about here. An elk-hide vest and carrying a couple of bags of gold-dust.'

There was complete silence in the saloon as the sheriff paused, then as if expecting some sort of action and not wishing to be caught up in it, such was the hard-nosed lawman's reputation, there was a general shuffling as people moved as far back as they could. The other players at the table stood up and joined the rest of the crowd at a safe distance.

'I'm guessing that description covers you, Mr Ethan Grant.'

The man at the table licked his lips and eyed his whiskey glass thoughtfully. Then:

'What's this arrest all about?'

15

'Thieving two bags of gold-dust,' replied the sheriff. 'And murder!'

'That's a damned lie. You couldn't know . . .'

A smile hovered over Sheriff Mat Hughes's lips.

'I couldn't know what? Sounds like a confession to me. Now get up and put your hands up.'

To everyone's surprise the suspect smirked and half-nodded his head. He began to rise.

'But maybe I don't want to be arrested, Sheriff.' He nodded at the sheriff's still-holstered weapon. 'How would you like to try taking my iron off me?'

Hughes stood stock still, his face displaying no emotion.

'My deputy is right behind you, Grant. Now put your hands up and don't be a fool.'

'Expect me to fall for that one,' the accused man said. And his hand moved with near lightning speed towards his gun. The sheriff instantly responded, but a shade slower. His eyes widened in alarm as he perceived that the man he planned to arrest had actually cleared leather and that his Navy Colt was rising, pointing at his chest, while his own draw was only half-made.

There was the explosion of a gunshot, and blood and brain-pulp erupted from a hole in the back of the suspect's head. His body swayed for a moment, and then fell forward onto the card table, which collapsed under his weight.

Sheriff Hughes stared aghast as two of the Clover Belles screamed in alarm and the other fainted. A murmur of shock ran around the saloon. Then relief showed in his face as he realized that he had stared death in the face. For the first time he had been outdrawn by another man. By rights it should have been him lying twitching on the floor instead of Ethan Grant.

'Good thing we didn't take any chances, huh, Sheriff,' said Burt Lister, the Dirtville deputy sheriff, blowing smoke from the barrel of his .45. 'Why do you figure he drew on you?'

Mat Hughes slowly shook his head.

'Desperation, I guess.'

But inwardly he felt confused. It wasn't supposed to happen like that.

It was the middle of the next afternoon when the Concord arrived in Dirtville. Clem Chambers, the driver, jumped down and landed on unsteady feet, before opening the door with a flourish. He hiccupped and grinned blearily.

'Dirtville folks, in all her glory. Hope you all enjoyed the ride,' he said, hopeful of a tip from at least one of the three dusty travellers.

'Three hours late! It's a disgrace,' growled a surly tobacco-salesman, as he stomped down the steps.

The second passenger, a middle-aged gentle-woman, a schoolmarm type, Clem presumed, was equally unimpressed.

'You're drunk! The first thing I'm going to do is find your employer and complain.'

Clem grinned toothlessly.

'Why, it sure was a pleasure driving you, ma'am,' he replied with whiskey-fuelled geniality. The lady departed with a huff of disgust.

'Here driver, this is for you,' came a mellow voice from inside. It was followed by the appearance of the handsomest woman Clem had ever seen. She was dressed smartly in a suit of light blue, with a matching toque that barely covered her corn-yellow tresses. She handed him a couple of dollars. 'Now can you direct me to the sheriff's office? I'm going to need his help.'

Clem was staring disbelievingly at the generous tip when anxiety crept into his muddled brain. 'You . . . you ain't gonna complain about me to the law, are you, ma'am? It wasn't my fault that—'

But she put a placating hand on his arm and smiled. It was a smile that melted the heart of the whiskey-soaked driver.

'I just need to see the sheriff,' she said.

Clem pocketed the money with alacrity, and then picked up her single small case, fending off a group of enthusiastic urchins as he did so, and led her across the square to the sheriff's office. Being none too fond of brushes of any kind with the law, he pushed open the door, laid her case down and tipped his hat.

'Hope he helps you real good,' he said, before returning to his waiting Concord and team.

Sheriff Mat Hughes was not in his office, but Deputy Burt Lister was. He was sitting in the sheriff's chair, his feet upon the desk, lovingly polishing his Remington .45 when he saw the woman cross the threshold. His eyes strayed over her features and curves and a slightly lascivious leer played across his lips.

'Well now, what can I do for you, ma'am?' he asked after a pause that made her squirm inside.

'Are you the sheriff?' she asked.

Burt Lister shot to his feet, holstering his weapon and throwing the rag he had been using on the desk.

'I'm his deputy, ma'am. And in his absence I'm in charge,' he replied pompously. 'Any problem, I'm the man to sort it for you.'

She shivered involuntarily. There was something about the young man that repulsed her. A mental image flashed through her mind of a rattlesnake moving in on a frightened jackrabbit, its cold reptilian face relishing its prey's helplessness. She felt herself flushing.

'I'm looking for a man,' she said.

The grin on the deputy's face broadened.

'Like I said, ma'am, I reckon I can solve any problem you have.'

She felt her initial dislike for the deputy suddenly heighten.

'I think perhaps it would be best if I wait until the sheriff returns. I would like him to help me find someone. It's important.'

Burt Lister sensed the girl's obvious antipathy towards him. She was about twenty years old, just a few years younger than himself. A man used to having women of a certain class fawn over him, he felt a sudden anger rise in his craw. This woman, he knew, felt that she was superior to him. Suddenly, he wanted to belittle her, to bring her down a peg in any way that he could.

'The sheriff may not be back for a couple of days,

ma'am,' he lied. 'If you've got this feller's name maybe I can help.'

She hesitated for a few moments before deciding that she couldn't afford to wait that long.

'His name is Grant. Ethan Grant,' she volunteered.

'Ethan Grant,' he repeated, as if he was trying to bring the name to mind. Then he clicked his tongue and nodded his head. 'I guess you're in luck, ma'am.' He crossed to the door and held it open for her. If you'd care to follow me, I reckon I can take you right to him.'

Abe Gibson and Zach Holmes were sitting on their regular chairs on the boardwalk outside the Dead Ringer saloon, smoking cigars and drinking coffee, when they saw Burt Lister escorting the young woman along the street towards the cemetery.

'Now what the hell is that young jasper doing with a looker like that?' Abe Gibson pondered.

'And why's he taking her over to Boot Hill!' Zach exclaimed.

Abe sucked air between his lips. 'Danged if I know, but it don't seem right.' He stood up and signalled Zach to follow suit. 'I reckon we ought to tag along, just in case. I've got a bad feeling about this.' And leaving their coffees unfinished they stepped down into the dusty Dirtville street and began to follow at a distance.

The woman spun round, fury written across her face.

'Is this some sort of sick joke!' she demanded.

Burt Lister took off his hat with deliberate slowness and ran a hand through his hair. He raised his eyebrows in mock surprise.

'A joke, ma'am? No joke here. You wanted me to take you to Ethan Grant and I've done it. We planted him this morning, just as soon as Doc Tolson had him ready.'

Her face suddenly drained of colour and went alabaster pale as she looked down at the freshly made mound of earth above the grave. Only then did the crude cross with its even cruder makeshift message register with her.

ETHAN GRANT – THIEF, MURDERER
SHOT DEAD MAY 26 1885

A hand went to her mouth and she visibly trembled.

Abe and Zach saw her distress and both hurried forward.

'What's that young fool done?' Abe cursed. But before they had taken more than a few paces the woman seemed to recover herself.

'Who ... who shot him?' she asked, her voice weak, barely more than a whisper.

Burt Lister grinned.

'He was a murdering dog and he tried to shoot the sheriff,' he explained, enjoying her obvious shock. 'Luckily I was there to save him.' He puffed out his chest pompously. He looked at her with an unpleasant, lopsided grin. 'But you haven't said why you wanted to find him.'

Her lips trembled and tears welled up in her eyes

as she fumbled for something in her drawstring purse.

'You . . . you shot Ethan?' Again, she trembled visibly, her hand rising from her purse, clutching a small silver derringer. She pointed it at the deputy's chest. 'Ethan Grant was my – fiancé!' she said, her voice choking with emotion.

Burt Lister's eyebrows shot heavenwards.

'That I didn't know – I couldn't have known, ma'am.' He raised his hands above his head. 'It – it wasn't anything – personal. D . . . don't shoot.'

Her lips curled contemptuously. She straightened her arm, cocking the derringer's hammer.

'You killed Ethan!' she repeated, her voice wavering. 'And that means . . .' she gasped, tears blurring her eyes and streaming down her cheeks. 'That means . . .'

Lister stared at her, his usual bravado having partially evaporated. He shook his head and uncertainly took a step backwards. Zach Holmes, however, was not so uncertain.

'No, ma'am!' he yelled. 'Don't do anything foolish.'

Zach's cry seemed to break a spell. Her hand began to tremble and she shook her head.

'No, nothing foolish,' she said. 'I've no reason for anything now!' Her eyes now seemed to be looking not at Burt Lister, but through him, into the distance beyond. She raised her hand, slowly swivelling the derringer round until it was pointing at her temple. Her hand shook violently, the derringer waving unsteadily in her hand.

'My God! No!' yelled Abe.

There was an explosion and a spray of blood from the side of her head spattered over the cross with its crude message. Then, as if in slow motion, she pitched gracefully over the newly dug grave.

TWO

Dirtville, like so many south-western towns, was used to violent death. Recent killings were talked about for days, before slowly seeping into the anecdotage of the town. The shooting of Ethan Grant, however, was different, followed as it was by the mystery woman who claimed to be his fiancée, head-shooting herself. The whole affair was so unique that the good people of Dirtville feared that talk about it could reach legendary proportions and permanently taint the town's reputation. When that happened a place could either die out and become a ghost town, or boom into an Abilene or Dodge City.

Grover Wilkins was feeling particularly concerned as he sat sipping strong coffee in the office of his stage and haulage company. Across the desk from him Sheriff Mat Hughes smoked one of his usual quirlies while he explained the events of the previous day to Dirtville's wealthiest citizen. For Grover Wilkins was indeed a wealthy man; the owner of the local bank, his own stage and haulage company as well as a half-dozen other concerns dotted around

24

the town. In all but name he owned the town.

'And you have no idea who the woman was?' he asked the lawman.

Mat Hughes shook his head and allowed a trail of smoke to escape from his lips.

'None, Mr Wilkins. But it just doesn't seem to fit. Ethan Grant was a no-count thief and killer, while she was . . .' he hesitated for a moment, 'a different class of person altogether.'

Grover Wilkins stroked his iron-grey moustache pensively. He was a tall, handsome man of middle years, a confirmed bachelor with the reputation of being as tough a businessman as could be found west of the Pintos. He took a pride in doing a job well and in gaining respect for the finished product, whether that was a new bank, a new stage or a donation to some local cause or other. And so, as one of the town's elders, he had a vision for the small south-western cow-town. That didn't include its gaining a dubious reputation for sensational crimes or shootings. Eventually, he slapped his desk and shook his head.

'I just can't believe it. Walt Burnett, my brother-in-law – murdered!'

Sheriff Hughes was in the act of stubbing out his cigarette. He stopped and stared in disbelief at Grover Wilkins.

'Your brother-in-law? I never knew that you had relatives in these parts.'

The Dirtville businessman shrugged his shoulders.

'No reason you should know, Sheriff,' he replied. 'Walt's ranch is fifty miles away. Not a lot of folk know that it actually belongs to me, or that Walt was just a tenant. He married my little sister and she stayed with me while he was away at the war.' He tapped below his knee and a hollow sound rang out from his artificial leg.

'When I was a youngster I thought of myself as kind of unlucky to have a horse land on me and crush the leg bones to a pulp, but it kept me out of the war. Anyway, I just about brought their son, Cole Burnett up for his first five years. When his pa came back I had just about had enough of ranching and wanted to try my hand at other things, so we came to an arrangement and I let Walt rename the ranch the Rocking WB, even though I still held the deeds.'

He produced a dilapidated old pouch and started stuffing thick-cut tobacco into the charred bowl of a large curled pipe. He applied a match. 'And the thing is, I was expecting Cole to show up any day now. He was going to show me some gold samples.'

'Gold?' Sheriff Hughes repeated.

Grover Wilkins gave a curt nod and tamped down the smouldering tobacco in his pipe with a thumb. 'That's right. Young Cole had been away for three or four years. He always was a headstrong kid and he had a fall-out with his pa. Anyway, he seemed to drift around for a while then spent time learning about mining engineering up north. Damn me if he didn't come back home about six months ago and find gold in the hills back of the ranch. Walt financed a mine and the next thing I heard was that they're producing enough to make it seem like a worthwhile little venture.'

Mat Hughes whistled wonderingly, then raised his cup and sipped his coffee. Then, looking over the rim of the cup he asked:

'This Ethan Grant, did you know him?'

Grover tapped the mouthpiece of his pipe against his teeth.

'I know of him, that's all. He's the foreman of the Rocking WB. He was taken in by Walt when Cole wandered off. There seemed to be some mystery about where he came from and rumour had it that he had spent some time on the other side of the law. I heard that he had some skill with a gun.'

He struck a light to his pipe again and puffed reflectively for a few moments. 'The truth is that I hadn't been to the ranch since my sister died. It suited me to leave things be and let Walt run the ranch. Apart from that, my leg doesn't like too much travelling,' he explained, grimacing as if a sudden pain had shot up the leg.

He rubbed his knee, then continued: 'Anyway it was clear that Walt didn't want too much probing, so I just assumed he must be some distant relative of Walt's. I do know that Walt made him foreman of the ranch and I hear tell that he made a pretty fair job of it.' He smoked some more, then: 'It doesn't seem to tally that he'd up and kill his – meal ticket,' he said, selecting his words with care.

'Well, I didn't know his history,' returned the sheriff. 'I do know that he was a nasty piece of work when he got himself fired up with whiskey.' He recounted his confrontation with Ethan Grant in the Dead Ringer saloon. 'He was about the fastest with a gun

27

that I ever saw. He outdrew me,' he confessed, blowing smoke between narrowed lips, 'I'd be dead if it hadn't been for my deputy, Burt Lister.' He sipped more coffee, then continued: 'Grant was carrying two bags of gold-dust with him. He tried using one as collateral to fund his poker-game. I guess that kind of clinches it, doesn't it.'

Grover Wilkins nodded agreement. 'Guess so. Now what about this fiancée? Have you any leads on who she was?'

Hughes shook his head. 'Not yet. It's all a mystery. I telegraphed George Veech, the constable at Hagsworth, and he knows nothing about any fiancée.' He struck a light to a fresh quirly he had just constructed between practiced fingers. 'But rest assured, Mr Wilkins,' he said rising to his feet. 'I'm sure as hell going to find out.'

Abe Gibson had felt sick to his stomach at the events of the last day or two. He had been shocked by the killing of Ethan Grant in his saloon. Clearing the place up after all that blood and brain-pulp had been plastered over the floor had been bad enough, but then the Clover Belles had packed up and left, which he couldn't blame them for. All in all, he had no choice but to close the place to get it cleaned up, which was a problem in itself since staying closed for too long would be bad for business. Drinkers needed to drink and loyalty seemed a short-lived quality in the south-west. But the more he thought about it, the more he was disturbed by the attitude of the young deputy, Burt Lister.

He's got a sadistic side to him, he thought to himself as he nudged his roan up the low trail that led through the Pintos network of canyons. He had felt the need to escape from Dirtville for a few hours at least, so he had headed off with his old Ballard sporting rifle, in the hope of maybe bagging a couple of jackrabbits.

But the image of that young woman falling over the grave and her blood splattering over her fiancé's grave-marker kept intruding upon his consciousness.

'Dammit!' he said out loud to the back of his roan's head. 'It's not as if I knew either of them!'

But again he came back to the cruel grin he had seen on the deputy's face. And he'd seen it twice. The first time had been just after he had shot Ethan Grant in the back of the head, when he'd suggested to Mat Hughes that it had been lucky for him that he'd been there. The second time had been after they'd carried the young woman's body away. Although he'd been within an inch of his life when she had pointed that derringer at him, he'd actually seemed to relish his flirtation with death and the run-up to that moment. It seemed as if he'd enjoyed goading her. And the more Abe thought about it the more it seemed that that had been the case. Although he had explained that she had come to the sheriff's office asking for help to find Ethan Grant, he had surprised everyone by taking her to the grave straight away.

'Surely any half-decent feller would have sat her down and explained what had happened,' Abe said again to the roan, as if he needed to give voice to his thoughts, to commune with someone, even if that was a critter that he was forcing up the dusty, red-hot canyon trail. 'Yessir, that is one sadistic bastard.'

He took his hat off and wiped his forehead. And in doing so he was distracted from his musings by the sight of a brace of turkey vultures circling high up a little distance away, soaring on the air currents.

'They've got something near to death in their sights,' he told the roan, instinctively feeling disgust for the bald-headed scavengers that waited until life had expired from their prey before going in to tear flesh from bone. He thought of raising his Ballard skywards and letting one of them have it. The rifle's .38 cartridges would bring one down, if he hit it, but he thought better of it in an instant. That critter that was so near death could be a wounded mountain lion or a coyote, so it could be mighty dangerous. A charging mountain lion would need dispatching fast, and the Ballard was only a single-shot weapon. So, making sure that his Peacemaker was fully loaded and ready for drawing from its holster, he primed his sporting rifle and nudged the roan with his knees to advance up the trail towards the spot where the vultures circled.

From the moment he regained consciousness, the man felt as if his whole body was broken. His head ached as if it had been hit with a sledge-hammer, his clothes were torn to tatters and he was cut and bruised all over from the buffeting he had received from his all too obvious descent to the bottom of the canyon from the high trail. Cactus spines were

30

wedged deep in his skin and his face felt as if someone had gone over it with a horseshoe rasp. And
indeed, as he looked up and saw the broken tangles
of mesquite and sagebrush, he silently thanked them
for having partially broken his fall. And because of
that, the overwhelming thought that burst into his
mind was the realization that he was still alive. It was
only after digesting this information that his numbed
mind began work on the simplest of questions, such
as who he was and where he was?

Then his mind conjured up the image of the man
whom he had befriended.

The bastard!

The reality of his predicament was emphasized in
no uncertain manner as the sun beat down on his
hatless head. The heat was scorching and he knew
that he was in danger of being cooked like an egg on
a griddle unless he moved. The main problem,
however, was that moving proved to be difficult. Yet
he managed to crawl, to drag himself towards the
shadow of the rocks. He thought that if he could just
get some water, sleep in the shade until the sun lost
its ferocity, then he might get his strength back.

There was no water to be found, but with some
difficulty he managed to break off a small piece of
cactus and pulp it sufficiently enough on rock to get
a mouthful of moisture. Its bitter taste made him feel
slightly nauseus, but he forced himself to swallow, for
any fluid was better than none and could mean the
difference between survival and death.

And as if to keep his mind concentrated on that
issue, he caught sight of a pair of turkey vultures

circling high overhead. Exhausted though he was, feeling the need to sleep, he grabbed a couple of jagged stones. He knew that any weapon at all was better than none if those flying scavengers had him high on their dinner menu.

The boom of a rifle echoed round the canyon for a few seconds before the body plummeted earthwards to land with a sickening thud, mere yards away from the man. He instinctively looked up and saw with relief that the other vulture had suddenly been dissuaded and was flying off in search of other food and probably also another mate. He had been all too aware of the fact that the vultures had been slowly spiralling downwards, ever nearer him.

Now who the hell did that? he thought. He pushed himself unsteadily to his feet and saw a man on a roan approach, a rifle cradled in his arms. Then he felt his head spin and his legs began to buckle under him. He slumped to the ground and passed out.

When he woke some time later the first thing he noticed was the aroma of a bird roasting over a fire of mesquite branches. He was propped up against a boulder and his face and arms stung like hell. He squinted in the sun, despite the shade, and saw a middle-aged man squatting on the other side of the fire, tending the roasting bird.

'Howdy, mister, looks like you took a tumble,' said Abe. 'You needed to sleep, too. You've been out for the count for the better part of an hour. Time enough for me to pluck this bird and get it roasting.' Abe prodded the bird with a forked stick, then touched his chest. 'My name's Gibson, Abe Gibson.'

The man nodded. 'I appreciate you killing that vulture. Are you planning to eat him?'

Abe grinned. 'If you've never tried turkey vulture you're in for a rare treat. Good strong meat, that's what you need, son.' He pointed the stick at the side of the canyon and the trail of broken cacti and sagebrush. 'I see where you came down. You sure are lucky to be alive, I reckon.'

'Yeah, well that's no thanks to the murdering varmint that slugged me and threw me over the edge. Least, that's what I figure happened.'

Abe handed him his canteen and pointed at a makeshift bandage that he had wound round a deep gash on the young man's forearm.

'I tried cleaning up some of those cuts and got most of the dirt out, but I guess we'd best get you seen by a doctor before too long. No bones broken as far as I can tell, but you need to be sure. Meanwhile, there's still plenty of water there, so you best get some inside you.'

While the younger man drank Abe started cutting chunks of meat from the vulture carcass.

'Where were you headed?' he asked.

'Dirtville,' replied the other. 'I have some business to do there.'

Abe grinned as he handed some roast turkey vulture on a stick.

'No plates, I'm afraid. You'll need to eat like the good Lord meant you to, with fingers.' He deliberately refrained from asking what sort of business, for it was the sort of question that men could be cagy about. Instead, he volunteered: 'I live in Dirtville. I run the Dead Ringer saloon.'

'This'll be my first trip to Dirtville. Is it a peaceful town?'

'It was,' replied Abe, with a mouthful of meat. 'Up until the day before yesterday. Then we had a killing. A man drew on our sheriff in my very own saloon.' He shook his head distastefully, then waved his hand with the bird-meat in the other's direction. 'You ought to try this meat, mister. It's good if I say so myself. That bird wasn't too old.'

The other looked doubtful, but raised his portion to lips and tore off a mouthful with strong white teeth.

'By the state of your clothes, that bushwhacker cleaned you out,' Abe remarked.

The younger man smirked.

'He took my hat, vest and guns. I guess he also took my horse and belongings.' His expression suddenly changed to one of anger. 'But I'm going to get them all back, however long it takes!'

'I guess he must have had decent boots already,' said Abe, pointing at the torn and scratched pair on the man's feet. He watched as the man ran a hand unconsciously over his boots. Then he became aware of a look of determination flashing across the young man's face. He saw a hand dip into his right boot and come out again in an instant.

There was a ratchet noise and he found himself staring straight at the barrel of a cocked derringer.

34

'Don't move a muscle!' the young man hissed between grated teeth.

Abe's eyes widened in alarm as he saw the finger tighten on the trigger.

THREE

After the funeral four men stood over the plot of ground on the rise above the Rocking WB ranch house. There were two graves, one old, one fresh. The other mourners had respectfully taken their leave, either to get back to their work on the ranch, or to head back to town. It had been a large affair, for the rancher had been well-liked by his men and by the surrounding community.

Tears welled up for the first time in Cole Burnett's eyes.

'He didn't deserve this,' he said, his jaw firm and his teeth set. 'Killed by a knife in the back.'

Judge Arthur Hollister, stick-thin and with a well-groomed goatee beard and a scar that creased the corner of his right eye to give him a stern appearance, put a hand on Cole's shoulder.

'A good man is with his good wife, your mother.'

The Hagsworth priest, the Reverend Emmet Kirk, portly and round-faced with round iron-rimmed spectacles clutched his Bible to his chest and coughed politely.

'The Lord will have a reckoning with whoever did this dreadful thing. And now, Cole, I'm afraid that I must get back to town. I have the funeral of Hank Turner to take in an hour's time back in Hagsworth.' He looked questioningly at the young man, then asked, 'Will you be coming?'

Cole Burnett looked at him, as if coming out of a reverie.

'Oh, Hank! I guess I'll come and pay my respects over his grave when I'm next in town. I feel I need to stay with my ma and pa for a while.'

Constable George Veech, a tall lumbering ox of a man, clearly uncomfortable with being dressed in a suit, shuffled his feet.

'I best get back too, Cole. I've got to get ready to ride over to Dirtville and see the sheriff there. I've got to collect the things they found on Ethan Grant's body. Before I do that, though, I need to do some investigating. We had another murder last night.'

The other three men stared at him in amazement.

'Willard Cox, the telegrapher, was found in an alley by some cowboys on their way back from a drinking spree. His throat was cut.'

The preacher gasped and went deathly pale, looking as if he might faint on the spot. He crossed himself.

'Any idea who did it, Constable?' he asked.

'None as yet. Willard was a well-liked guy. A bit nosy, maybe, but that's the nature of the job, seeing other people's business.'

Cole Burnett shook his head sadly.

'There seems to be a cloud of evil passing over the

country. Does he have kin?'

The constable shook his head.

'That's some mercy anyways,' said Judge Hollister. 'Have you wired the other towns? Warned other telegraphers? Who knows what sort of lunatic is riding around.'

'That's another problem, Judge,' replied the constable. 'Hagsworth is damn well cut off. Before I came out here this morning, although I don't know much about telegraphy, I know enough to tell that whoever killed Willard Cox also cut the wires. So, until we get a replacement from the telegraph company and they fix the wires, I can't get in touch with any of the other lawmen around. As you all know, Dirtville is the nearest town and it's a day's ride away, either through the Pintos or by overland stage.'

Cole Burnett's steely grey eyes fixed on the constable.

'In that case, talking of Dirtville, I'll go and pick up that bastard Grant's things, Constable. They'll belong to us anyhow. In fact, I'm willing to bet he had two bags of gold-dust on him.'

The constable nodded his head.

'Sure enough. That's what the sheriff said in his telegram before the wire went down. And if you don't mind the ride, it would sure help me out. You don't see any legal problem with that, do you, Judge?'

Judge Hollister shook his head.

'If it's Cole's property it should be OK for him to collect it. I'm just sorry that I can't help in all of this. Walt Burnett was a good friend of mine and he did a

Christian thing in taking that young Grant feller under his wing. It's a pity that the Dirtville lawmen had to kill him.' He pointed his hat at Walt Burnett's grave. 'I would have considered it a pleasure to have tried him.'

The preacher and constable took their leave and Cole invited the judge into the ranch house for a drink. When they were sitting opposite each other in leather armchairs in the plush sitting-room, each with a whiskey glass in his hand, Cole asked:

'Why are you looking so worried, Judge?'

The judge sipped his drink, then smoothed moisture from his moustache.

'It's Laura. She's not been back to the house for a couple of days. I was in two minds about telling Constable Veech.' He took another hefty swig. 'For all the good that would do,' he added sarcastically.

'My God!' exclaimed Cole. 'We've got to do something, Judge. If anything happened to Laura—'

'I know, Cole. Ever since you came back from the North I've been hoping that you and she would tie the knot. In fact, the last time I saw her I assumed she was coming out here. She certainly rode off in this direction.'

Cole stood up and walked over to the decanter on the side table. He poured each another liberal measure.

'You don't know how pleased I am to hear you say that, Judge. It's been right in the front of my mind to speak to you soon. Laura and I have been getting real close. But I wonder where she could be, since she certainly didn't come here.'

'I guess she must have gone to visit one of her friends then,' Judge Hollister replied. 'She can be quite headstrong, I admit. I guess she'll show up later today.'

Cole raised his glass and sipped the warm liquor.

'Then I'll call on you both just as soon as I get back from Dirtville.' He smiled. Having the judge's blessing was certainly part of his plan.

As the constable and the preacher rode back to Hagsworth together, George Veech was also feeling rather uncertain. He had meant to ask Cole Burnett if he knew anything about Ethan Grant's having a fiancée. But the thought left his head a moment later when Emmet Kirk reached into his saddle-bag and produced a bottle of rye.

'Here's to old Walt Burnett,' said the preacher.

'Amen to that,' replied the constable, and they both laughed as they ambled along.

Already George Veech had decided that the question was of no importance.

Abe Gibson was dimly aware of a curious rattling noise, which was immediately obscured by the bark of the derringer. He lurched back as the percussion echoed round the canyon, and he landed on his back, blood splattering his bare forearm. Yet there was no pain.

'What the hell . . .' he gasped, struggling back up, his hand instinctively searching his bloodied arm for sign of a wound.

Smoke curled from the barrel of the derringer

and the stranger pointed to the ground about a yard to Abe's left. The body of a diamondback rattlesnake lay in the dust, its head a bloody pulp.

'I didn't think you were armed,' Abe said, shuffling away from the dead snake. 'Lucky for me that you were! Thanks, son.' He produced a handkerchief and distastefully wiped the snake's blood from his arm. Then he pointed to the derringer. 'Effective little devil, that,' he said. 'What is it, a .22?'

The young man handed the gun over for inspection. 'That's right, silver-plated, .22 calibre. It's one of a pair.'

At that Abe took the gun and inspected it. He thought that he had seen its like before – in the hand of the mystery woman who had shot herself. His mouth seemed to go dry all of a sudden as he looked the weapon over.

'Mister, would you mind telling me your name?'

For the first time the young man smiled. He held out his hand.

'Grant,' he replied. 'Ethan Grant. I'm sorry if I spooked you there, but there was no time to explain.'

Abe shook hands then passed the weapon back.

'I don't know how to tell you this, Ethan,' he said, reaching inside his vest for a couple of cigars. Ethan refused and Abe lit his from a mesquite ember from the fire. 'As far as everyone in Dirtville is concerned, you're a dead man, buried in Boot Hill yesterday.'

Ethan Grant clapped his knee in disgust.

'You mean that bastard who sandbagged me got himself killed? Damn! I wanted to settle my score

41

with him, myself.'

Abe described the clothes the other man had been wearing and Ethan confirmed them as his own.

'And he was carrying two bags of gold-dust. Apparently the constable of Hagsworth had telegraphed a message to our sheriff, Mat Hughes, saying you had killed two men and stolen gold. He was to arrest and detain you, but you – that is, the *hombre* they thought was you – got himself well liquored and drew on the sheriff. Unfortunately for him the deputy was standing behind him.' He blew smoke and looked at the glowing end of his cigar. 'It happened in my saloon,' he added distastefully.

Ethan regarded the saloon-owner through narrowed eyes.

'Who am I supposed to have killed?'

'Walt Burnett and a miner called Hank Turner.'

The effect of this news was amazing. Ethan Grant leapt to his feet and kicked the remains of the carcass of the roasted bird.

'That's a damned lie! I'd never have harmed a hair on Walt Burnett's head. He was like a father to me. And as for Hank Turner, I barely knew him. Cole Burnett brought him with him when he came back to the Rocking WB. Cole is Walt's son. A real prodigal son, but the apple of Walt's eye.'

'Do you know anything about this gold?'

Ethan was standing with his hands interlocked behind his head, then he shrugged and sat down again.

'I was given two bags of it by Cole and told to take it to Grover Wilkins in Dirtville. He's Walt's brother-

42

in-law. A banker and businessman in these parts, so I understand.'

'Brothers-in-law? I didn't know that, Ethan. Go on.'

'Cole gave me a letter from Walt to take to him. It's all to do with financing this mine of theirs out back of the Rocking WB. On my way this feller joined up with me. Said he was on his way to Dirtville as well, so we rode the high trail through the Pintos and stopped to eat and bed down. That's about all I can say, except that I woke up with a headache and with those damned vultures circling over me. I must have been out cold for a day or thereabouts.' He winced as he touched his head. 'Sure feels that way.'

'You still got this letter?'

Ethan patted his pockets, then snapped his fingers in recollection.

'I'll still have it if it didn't fall out of my other boot,' he said, bending and reaching inside. 'Here it is. I reckon that you'll be a good witness. Let's see what Walt wrote to his brother-in-law.'

He showed Abe the envelope before breaking the seal and opening it up.

'What the . . . he began, showing Abe two sides of a blank piece of paper. 'I guess I don't understand. Why would Walt send a blank paper to his brother-in-law?'

'You sure he did send it, Ethan? Didn't you say that his son Cole gave you it?'

'Yes, but that makes no sense.' Again, he interlocked his fingers behind his neck and stretched backwards, as if trying to break a kink in the muscles.

43

Abe pulled at his cigar, savoured the smoke then let out a slow stream.

'Do you get on well with Cole?'

Ethan shrugged. 'Always seemed to. Walt told me that I had to do my dangdest to get on with him. And when Walt asked me to do something, I did it. He was good enough to take me in when I landed on hard times.'

Abe noticed the young man's face cloud over in the vague way that he had seen so many times before when men wanted to gloss over a time in their life.

'He taught me all I know about ranching, and he made me his foreman a couple of years ago. I heard tell that Cole was always a tad wild and had gone off adventuring for a few years. Then about six months ago he came back all knowledgeable about mining. He brought Hank Turner with him and they set about surveying the section of hills outside the Rocking WB land. A couple of weeks ago they struck a mother lode and Walt registered it in Cole's name. I can't say I know much more than that, since ramrodding the Running WB takes most of the hours in the day.'

Abe knocked ash from the end of his cigar,

'Don't take this wrong, Ethan, but could Cole have any reason to – double-cross you? To set you up somehow.'

Ethan Grant swallowed hard. Mind if I take you up on that offer of a cigar,' he said. And a few moments later, with his cigar going to his satisfaction, he volunteered: 'Only thing I can think of is jealousy.'

'You mean a lady?'

Ethan's face softened. 'I have a lady-friend, yes. The sweetest girl that ever sat leather in these parts.'

Worry lines had deepened across Abe's brow.

'Tell me more.'

Ethan blew a puff of smoke, then helped himself to a swig of water from the canteen.

'Her name's Laura Hollister. She's my age and the prettiest girl for a hundred miles.' His eyes twinkled and his mouth creased into an infectious smile as he brought her image into his mind's eye. 'And she likes to get her own way', he added.

'Does Cole have any affections for her?'

Ethan bit his lip. 'I reckon so. At least Laura says that she doesn't like to be alone with him, and although she's polite to him she doesn't like his attentions. And I can understand that, because Cole has this wild streak. I guess if he wants a girl he won't beat about the bush. That's why we've been kind of secretive. She didn't want him to know about us.' He had been fiddling with a twig, twisting it round and round in his hands. With a sigh he snapped it in two and tossed it into the fire. 'But I think he knows, for all that. He sometimes tries to probe me.'

Abe became aware of a slightly nauseous feeling in the pit of his stomach. He suddenly lost the taste for his cigar and cast it into the fire.

'Love is a powerful emotion, son. You have any plans together?'

Ethan nodded. 'I reckon that we'll marry some day. Of course, I'd have to tell Walt.' His face suddenly clouded as he realized what he had said. 'I mean I would have had to tell Walt, and I'd have to talk to the judge.'

Abe Gibson was beginning to wish that he had never embarked on a discussion with this young man whom he had found at the bottom of the canyon. There was clearly double-dealing going on, and tragedy in plentiful supply.

'Ethan, did you two have any sort of understanding. Had you actually asked this young woman—'

'Had I asked her to marry me? Yes sir, and since we aimed to keep it all a secret for a while, we sort of bought each other an engagement gift.'

'You bought a pair of derringers and each took one,' Abe divined.

It was Ethan's turn to look surprised. 'How on earth did you guess that?' he asked.

Abe Gibson pushed himself to his feet and went across to his saddlebag, returning after a moment with a small bottle of brandy.

'Drink some of this, Ethan,' he said. 'I've got some bad news for you.'

And he recounted the events of Laura Hollister's coming to town and of her meeting with the Dirtville deputy, and the events at the grave of the man who had sandbagged Ethan.

Ethan had listened in stunned disbelief. He ran his hands through his thick black hair, his face suddenly drawn and etched with unbelievable sorrow.

'Laura's dead!' He shook his head and stood up. Then, with a choking voice: 'I've got to go and see her. She's not – not been. . . ?'

46

Abe stood up and put a hand on the young man's shoulder.

'No, she hasn't been buried. A couple of townsmen took her body to Doc Tolson's surgery. He does all the embalming in Dirtville.'

'When's the funeral? Have they let Judge Hollister know?'

Abe's eyes opened wide.

'Judge Hollister! So she's his daughter? He has a tough reputation in these parts. I guess he'll be devastated. But the thing is, Ethan, no one knew who she was, so no one will have told him.'

Ethan clenched his fists. 'That darned bushwhacker! If he hadn't put me out of action this probably wouldn't have happened.' His eyes almost seemed to burn like coals. 'And I guess me and that deputy will have a reckoning.'

'Now hold on, Ethan. Burt Lister is a young fool, I know, but he's a lawman. You can't go picking a fight with him. The first thing is to go and see the sheriff and let him know that you're the real Ethan Grant.'

'Abe, I thank you for all you've done for me today, but I've got a bad feeling about all of this. Cole gave me a letter and said that Walt wanted me to give it and the gold dust to Grover Wilkins. And now Walt is dead.' He shook his head. 'There's a double-cross going on at Dirtville and I mean to find out more before I let anyone know that I'm Ethan Grant.'

Abe Gibson nodded agreement.

'In that case, I guess the first thing we need to do is go see Doc Tolson.' He pointed to Ethan's tattered clothes. 'Lucky for you I carry a spare shirt in my

47

saddle-bag, so that you won't attract too much attention in Dirtville.'

Ethan nodded silently as he caught the shirt. At that moment he felt that he had to be master of his emotions. Grief and anger made two bad travelling companions.

FOUR

Mrs Martha Cusworth sat in the plain wooden chair in Dr Sam Tolson's consulting-room and winced as he applied a balm to the back of her hand before binding it with a linen bandage.

'That'll teach me to be more careful with that stove of mine,' she said with a smile, as the town doctor turned and made notes on a card on his desk.

'It'll be fine in a week, Martha,' Doc Tolson replied. 'You just have to keep burns like that dry and out of water.'

'Which as you know is difficult when you run an eatery like me,' she returned.

Sam Tolson clicked his teeth as he glanced at the good-looking widow. He was a tall, handsome man in his mid-forties with a full head of thick brown hair and a ready smile.

'Then perhaps you need to get Abe Gibson over to help you wash up at the end of the day,' he suggested, mischievously.

Martha Cusworth grinned back.

'The day I get Abe Gibson to do anything he doesn't want to will be a real red-letter day,' she returned.

Doc Tolson stood up and made for the door.

'Come on, Martha, the whole town knows that Abe is crazy about you. He's just shy, that's all.'

'He's too busy making money and drinking whiskey in that saloon of his, you mean.' She bit her lip. 'At least he was until that unpleasant business the other day. Today he's gone off hunting in the Pintos to try and take his mind off it.'

Before the doctor could put a hand on the door-handle there was a tap on the door and a beautiful, high-cheek-boned young woman with raven-black hair entered. She was dressed in a long dress of blue cotton, topped with a red velvet shirt and with an intricately woven sash of red and blue. She nodded to Martha and then made a silent gesture to the doctor.

'Good morning, Red Cloud,' Martha greeted, holding up her bandaged hand. 'I burned myself cooking this morning,' she explained. 'Sam has patched me up again. So now it's back to the stove. Woman's work is never done, eh?'

Red Cloud nodded, a light dancing in her eyes, yet she said nothing. And indeed, Martha Cusworth had not expected her to say anything, for few people in Dirtville ever heard the Navaho woman talk. Not even when she delivered babies, as she had done many times, since she and Sam Tolson had come to Dirtville. Despite that, she seemed able to convey her meaning with a mix of sign language and gestures, and most of the good folk of Dirtville assumed that she had been born mute. It was an impression that

50

the town doctor had never seen fit to correct. Bound as he was by the Hippocratic Oath, he never discussed patients with anyone, and he never indulged in gossip. He believed that people should be mindful of their own business, just as he was of his. At times this made people feel that he was aloof, but if he was aware of it, he never seemed to mind one bit.

'Ah, I see,' Sam Tolson said, catching Red Cloud's unspoken hand-gesture. 'I have to go now, Martha. Please drop by in four days and let me see that hand again.'

The widow smiled. 'And then maybe one day I could cook a meal for you two and Abe.' She smiled at the idea.

'That would be fine, Martha,' replied Sam Tolson. 'What do you think, Red Cloud?'

'It will be good,' Red Cloud said, her face still impassive.

Martha smiled, pleased to be one of the few honoured friends who enjoyed any dialogue at all with Red Cloud.

'Yes, dinner, the four of us, after I close up some day, that's an excellent idea.' And she made her way out past them through the now empty waiting-room.

Dr Sam Tolson, Physician, Surgeon and Embalmer, as the sign outside his surgery proclaimed, had led a rich and varied life before settling in Dirtville. Like most men of his generation he had served in the War and had felt tainted by it. Honourable discharge at the end of hostilities had been a relief from the patching up of maimed and badly wounded young men, from the epidemics of dysentery and cholera and from the awful realization that man was capable of incredible acts of inhumanity to his fellows. It had sickened him to his core and as a result he spent a few years living an itinerant's life, stopping at towns or villages just long enough to minister to the really sick, or to help whatever baby needed some help getting into the world, but never staying long enough to get too used to the people. It wasn't that he didn't like his fellow human beings; it was just that the loss of friends during the War had made him wary of getting too fond of people. Until he himself got sick.

It had happened during one of his wandering spells, when he had gone off into the wilderness in search of medicinal herbs and a little bit of peace and quiet. A fall from his horse, a gash on the leg and its subsequent infection led to him holing up in a cave and lying delirious for more days than he cared to imagine. That he had come close to death was clear, as was the realization that, left to its own devices, his leg would have gone gangrenous.

It had been providential that a hunting party of Navaho Indians found him and took him back to their village, where some real healing was performed on him by Running Buffalo, the tribe's medicine-man. It was during his long convalescence, as he learned about Navaho medicinal herbs from Running Buffalo, and in turn taught him about simple surgical techniques, that he fell in love with and was given as a wife, Red Cloud, the medicine-man's daughter.

They stayed six months with his new-found family before the desire for some sort of 'civilization' urged him to seek pastures new with his new young wife. They travelled further south until eventually they hit the town of Dirtville, where he rented rooms and set up his plate.

'Any problems?' he asked, once Martha Cusworth had closed the outer door.

Red Cloud shook her head and again put a cupped hand to her lips, in the sign of food. Sam Tolson laughed and bent down to kiss her full lips.

'How lucky I am to have you looking after me.'

She nodded her head ever so slightly.

'Red Cloud knows,' she replied softly, and taking his hand led him through to the back of the house.

Zach Holmes was having a busy but unproductive day. Everyone in town and their dog had seemed to want to send telegrams, and they were all frustrated when he gave them the same message.

'The line's down somewhere between here and Hagsworth. Just leave your message and as soon as I can get through, I'll send a boy to let you know.'

But it worried him because, unless communication was established soon, he was going to have to do it the hard way. And that meant packing up the repair tackle and following the line back. It was time that he could ill afford. And no one was interested in his problems; they just wanted their business sorting out. To them all he was polite and reassuring that the wire would soon be ready. Yet he had a bad feeling about it. There seemed to be something odd about the recent messages from Hagsworth, the shootings, then a dead line. He wondered if Willard Cox, his counterpart in Hagsworth, was having just as bad a time as he was.

He smiled to himself as he thought of Willard preparing to ride the line the next day. It would make a good yarn if they met half-way along the wire. They could maybe have a drink as they fixed the line. He made a mental note to pack a bottle of redeye. As he mused over this prospect he looked out of the window and saw Sheriff Mat Hughes strolling up the street. It struck him as curious that the Dirtville lawman didn't seem too concerned about not being able to telegraph out.

It was mid-evening by the time Abe and Ethan made it to town. They'd taken turns of riding the roan and both were feeling leg-weary. By the time they'd fed, watered and bedded the animal down exhaustion had pretty near overcome them.

'Where's the doctor's place?' Ethan asked, as they left the livery.

Another voice answered instead of Abe's.

'What you need to see the doc for? You ain't ill, are you, Abe?'

Abe peered into the shadows and grinned as Zach Holmes stepped off the boardwalk and came towards them.

'Dammit, Zach, what you prowling around in the dark for? I figured you'd be over in the Dead Ringer by now.'

The telegrapher shook his head.

'I'm giving it a miss tonight. I've got to head out to check on the wire. It's gone dead between here and Hagsworth.'

At this news Ethan and Abe exchanged suspicious glances. Then Zach noticed Ethan's battered and bruised face and the torn trousers, and looked quizzically at his friend. Abe patted Zach's arm and smiled at Ethan.

'This is my best friend, Zach Holmes, the local telegrapher. He may look like the sort of cuss who'd gossip, but he's a straight shooter. Would you mind if'n I tell him who you are?'

Ethan bit his lip. 'I reckon that'd be OK, Abe, as long as we tell him in private.'

Zach held out a hand and they shook.

'Sounds mysterious, sure enough. I reckon the best place for a chinwag would be Martha Cusworth's Eatery. She's closed for the day, but she's already said I could get a bite. Care to join me?'

Ethan hesitated. 'But the doctor's?'

Abe put a comforting hand on the young man's shoulder.

'I figure food and a hot drink would build your strength up a bit, son. Then I'll take you over myself.'

Ethan nodded and let himself be guided across the street to the said Widow Cusworth's Eatery. A knock on the door was answered after a few moments by the door curtain being pulled back and the proprietor unbolting and opening the door when she recognized Abe and Zach.

'Any chance of feeding two more, Martha?' Abe asked, hopefully.

And clearly, Martha Cusworth's face had fairly lit up on seeing Abe Gibson.

'Of course, anything for a friend,' she said, as she stepped back and ushered them all in before closing and bolting the door again. Then as Ethan stepped into the lamplight, she gasped upon seeing his face and his tattered clothing. 'My goodness, what happened to your friend?'

Ethan gave her a half-hearted lopsided grin.

'I kind of fell down a canyon, ma'am. Cactus and scrub ripped me to pieces and Mr Gibson here was kind enough to shoo off a couple of vultures that had me all marked up as dinner.'

'In that case the first thing you need is a wash and some clean clothes. I've got the water all ready boiling and if you don't mind, I can get you some fresh clothes. You're about the same size as my late husband.' And without more ado she took his hand and hustled him off to her living-quarters. 'In the meanwhile,' she called over her shoulder, 'you two help yourselves to coffee. It's freshly made.'

Twenty minutes later, Ethan let himself into the restaurant where Abe and Zach were sitting at a corner table, which was draped with a neat red-and-white-checked tablecloth and with four places set out. Steam rose from bowls of freshly cooked vegetables and a mouth-watering aroma of cooking filled the air.

'Well, lookee there,' Abe said with a grin. 'The boy scrubs up pretty well. Come and sit down, Ethan.'

'Ethan?' Zach repeated, in some surprise, for he and Abe had been talking of other matters while he washed.

At that moment Martha Cusworth returned with a great pot of antelope stew.

'Settle down now and we'll soon be ready.' She began serving food. 'Did I hear that your name is Ethan?' she asked.

'That's right ma'am. My name is Ethan Grant.'

The news produced started expressions on both Zach's and Martha's faces. Abe urged him on with a nod and the fact that he was among friends. And so, while they all ate, Ethan recounted the events that had brought him to Dirtville. Zach and Martha listened in amazement.

'You poor thing,' Martha whispered, upon hearing about Ethan and Laura being engaged. She bit her lip. 'I'm so sorry, Ethan.'

'Are you going to go to the sheriff and let him know that you're the real Ethan Grant?' Zach asked, as Martha poured coffee for them all.

'Not yet,' Ethan replied. 'I reckon I need to stop and have a good think. Sleep on it.'

'You'll stay with me at the Dead Ringer,' Abe announced.

Ethan smiled. 'I'm obliged, Abe. And maybe you could see your way to helping me acquire a gunbelt.'

Martha Cusworth looked worried.

'Will that be necessary? There seems to have been so much violence in Dirtville already?'

Ethan shook his head. 'I don't know anything much at the moment, ma'am,' he replied. 'All I really want to do right now is see Laura's body. I need to pay my respects.'

Abe had been about to strike a light to a cigar, but

thought better of it. He put it back inside his vest.

'Come on Ethan, let's both go and pay our respects.'

Red Cloud tossed her head back and gave a long moan of pleasure before bending and kissing Sam passionately.

'You really are the most lovely woman I ever met,' the town doctor said a few moments later as they lay side by side in bed.

'I know,' she replied with a smile that melted his heart. Their bed was the one place where Red Cloud ever became anything like vocal. Indeed, she was wanton. 'And you are almost as good a medicine-man as Running Buffalo, my father.'

'Why you. . . . !' he said as he began tickling her, sending her into squeals of laughter.

Then they heard the insistent knocking at the front door. Sam made to get up, but he was pushed back against the pillows by two surprisingly strong hands.

'Red Cloud will get rid of them,' she said, slipping out of bed and pulling on a doeskin dress. 'A good medicine-man needs his strength!' she whispered with a smile as she tied her hair back. 'I will be back soon,' she added, raising her eyebrows suggestively.

Sam grinned despite himself.

'But it could be an emergency,' he protested.

'Red Cloud will decide,' she replied, leaving the room with the grace of a cat.

But the sight of Abe Gibson's solemn face and the fact that he was accompanied by a handsome but battered young man alerted some sixth sense within her and she realized that the town doctor would be needed. She held the door open for them to come in.

'I'm truly sorry about disturbing the doc at this hour,' Abe said, as she closed the door behind them, 'but this is Ethan Grant. We've come to pay our respects to his fiancée. Could you ask the doctor if we could see her body?'

Red Cloud held out a hand and gestured for them to go through to the waiting-room. But Sam Tolson's voice came through the hallway door and he stepped in, tying the sash of his dressing robe.

'I thought I heard your voice, Abe,' he said, his face registering surprise. 'But did I hear you rightly? Did you say that this is Ethan Grant? And if so, then who. . . ?'

'You heard him right, Doc,' said Ethan, extending a hand. 'I'm Ethan Grant and the man in the town cemetery is a thieving bushwhacker that I met the other night.'

Sam shook hands and pointed to Ethan's bruised and cut face.

'Maybe you better let me look at your injuries, Mr Grant.'

But Ethan shook his head, tears welling up in his eyes.

'I'd really just appreciate seeing Laura's body.'

Again the doctor's face registered surprise.

'By body, I assume that you are referring to the lady who shot herself by the grave of . . .' he hesitated, then corrected himself, 'the grave of the man she thought was her fiancé.'

It was Abe's turn to look perplexed. 'What are you driving at, Doc?'

The town doctor took a step towards a door and put his hand on the handle.

'I'm saying that I don't have a body, but I do have one very ill, but live patient.'

FIVE

After swiftly telling the doctor about his relationship with Laura and about his own narrow escape from death, Ethan followed the doctor through to the spare bedroom.

'Laura! My God!' Ethan gasped, taking in the appearance of the girl lying on the bed, the crown of her head swathed in heavy bandages, her face and lips deathly pale. For a moment he thought that she was dead, she was so still.

Doc Tolson lifted the unconscious woman's wrist and felt her pulse. Then he gently raised her right eyelid and inspected the pupil of her eye. He turned with a reassuring smile.

'She's weak, Ethan, but she's doing as well as can be expected.'

Tears welled up in Ethan's eyes. 'Has – has she regained consciousness at all, Doc?'

Sam Tolson shook his head.

'Not yet, but I remain hopeful.' He placed a hand on the younger man's shoulder. 'But I'd be failing in my duty if I didn't tell you that every day that goes by without her coming round makes it less likely that she will do.'

Ethan's eyes registered near panic and he made as if to rush to his fiancée's side. But the doctor held him back with a gently restraining arm.

'Not yet, Ethan. Hearing your voice might help. I've seen it happen before, but it's late now and it's not a natural time to rouse someone. Tomorrow will be time enough.'

Ethan sighed with a nod of resignation as he accepted the town doctor's professional opinion. He allowed himself to be guided back into the sitting-room where Abe and Red Cloud sat waiting.

'Damn me, Doc,' said Abe, rising from a chair with a glass of whiskey in his hand. 'I almost fainted myself when you told me that the young lady was still alive! How come you kept it a secret?'

Sam Tolson gave a wan smile as he poured whiskey into two glasses and handed one to Ethan.

'I've kept no secrets, Abe. I have a duty of care to my patient and that means I have to treat her details and her progress as confidential. This young lady was brought to me after she had shot herself. The fact that everyone in town seems to have assumed that she had killed herself is nothing to do with me.'

'But I saw her shoot herself in the head at point-blank range,' protested Abe. He looked hesitantly at Ethan, then: 'I saw the blood, then she fell.'

'That's as maybe,' returned Sam,' but I'm guessing that her hand was shaking when she pulled the trigger. Anyway, that bullet just glanced across her temple. Oh, it made a nasty enough-looking wound, and it caused a depressed fracture of her skull, but it didn't actually penetrate into her brain. She was alive all right.'

Red Cloud took a pace forward and put a loving hand on Sam's arm.

'Doctor Tolson opened her head,' she said matter-of-factly. 'He lifted the bone and let the clot out.'

Ethan's face went as pale as alabaster. He gulped his whiskey, then:

'You operated on her?'

Doc Tolson nodded. 'I operated on dozens of young men with head injuries during the War. When I examined her I knew that she had some pressure under the depressed fracture. That means that she had bled under the fracture and the clot was putting pressure on the brain. Once the clot was removed the pressure was relieved.'

Ethan swallowed hard. 'And will she. . . ?'

'Will she pull round?' Doc Tolson finished. 'I hope so, Ethan. Red Cloud made a poultice to help her scalp wound heal and we're managing to get some herbal medicines into her in the form of liquid.'

'Herbs?' Ethan repeated.

The town doctor nodded. 'That's right. My drugs are pretty nigh useless for unconscious patients, but I've seen incredible results with Navaho herbal medicine. Red Cloud's father is one of the wisest medicine-men I've ever seen.'

Ethan slowly nodded his head.

'It's all been a shock, Doc. I'm just so grateful that she's at least got a chance. Is there anything that I can do to help?'

Doc Tolson gestured towards the clock. 'I think the best thing you could do is to get some sleep. Come back tomorrow and see if talking to her will lift her out of this coma.'

Ethan rose and shook the doctor's hand,

'Well, let's get you that sleep,' said Abe, rising and placing his empty glass on the table. Then he turned to the doctor.

'Should we tell people that the lady is alive?' he asked.

The doctor shook his head.

'Like I said, Abe, I never breach a confidence without the patient's say-so. And as yet I haven't had this patient's go-ahead.'

Ethan nodded. 'I think we should keep it that way too, Doc. I've a feeling that the fewer people who know the better. For now at least.'

Abe was up bright and early as usual in order to supervise the clearing up of the saloon and the preparation for the custom of the day ahead. The aroma of ham and eggs and freshly brewed coffee enticed him into the back kitchen where he found Ethan sitting down to a full plate, courtesy of Rufus, Abe's elderly cranky cook.

'Got your appetite back, I'm glad to see,' Abe said with a grin as he sat down opposite him at the deal table. He helped himself to coffee and waved away Rufus's offer of a similar serving. 'No thanks, Rufus. I'm heading over to Martha's Eatery in a while.' Then seeing the crestfallen expression on Rufus's face, he added: 'No offence, but I've got some business I need to talk over with her.'

Rufus ran a hand over his head with its short, grizzled grey and ginger hair, then winked at Ethan.

'I'm guessing you're meaning you got some courting business in mind, eh, boss?'

Abe made a mock move to throw his cup at his employee.

'I reckon you'd best get out to that bar and give the boys some of this dishwater you call coffee. It'd be a good thing if some of you escaped jail-birds could keep awake long enough to give a decent day's work once in a while.'

Rufus grabbed the coffee-pot and stomped out with good-natured mock chagrin.

'Whatever Abe says, Rufus,' Ethan said with a grin, 'You sure as hell cook a fine breakfast.'

Rufus nodded appreciatively as he stood with a hand on the doorknob.

'And you sure are welcome, Mr Kincaid. It's kinda unique to have anyone appreciate you round here.'

A few moments later, when they were alone Abe said:

'So, Mr *Kincaid*, I see you've got old Rufus eating out of your hand.'

Ethan pushed his plate aside with a sigh of satisfaction.

'I figured it would be best to introduce myself as Zeke Kincaid, your new piano-player. Hope you don't mind.'

Abe grinned back. 'Fine by me, Ethan. But how come you knew I didn't have a piano-player already? Or that I even had a piano.'

Ethan took a sip of coffee. 'I did a little recon-noitring first thing this morning. I saw your piano, a damn fine model, but it didn't take a professor of music to know that it hasn't been played for at least six months. I would have tuned it then, but I reck-oned the neighbourhood might have complained.'

Abe slapped the table, then held out his hand.

'Welcome then, Zeke. It's just a pity that you didn't come round a day or two earlier, that way I wouldn't have lost my performance act, the Clover Belles,' he said wistfully. Then with eyebrows rising suspiciously, 'I take it you really know how to play?'

Ethan grinned. 'Oh I've picked up a few skills along the way. I may not be up to playing in a fancy concert-hall, but I reckon I know enough tunes for a run-down saloon like the Dead Ringer.'

For a moment Abe stared at the younger man, not quite sure how to take him. Then he snorted as he caught the twinkle in Ethan's eye.

'In that case, when you've finished feeding your face, how about we get some other duds to make you look something more like a piano-player and less like a hobo.'

The final transformation of Ethan Grant into Zeke Kincaid took place upstairs in Abe's spare room. A huge wardrobe contained all manner of clothes left over the years by various customers, either through drunken carelessness or in payment of gambling debts or bar bills. From it Ethan selected a gaudy yellow-and-green-striped waistcoat and a battered derby hat.

'A regular key-slammer,' Abe said with a laugh.

'Well boy, you look the part; I just hope that you aren't joshing me about your playing. I've got a lot of customers who might shoot off a couple of fingers or toes if they don't like the sound of your piano-plonking.'

Ethan adjusted the derby hat at an angle so that the narrow brim concealed a couple of the grazes on his brow.

'I liked my own hat and vest better. They were both kinda unique.'

Abe sucked air between his teeth.

'Unique maybe, but tainted now. They were buried with . . . the body.'

Ethan nodded dispassionately, turning his head one way then the other to study his bruised and gashed reflection in the mirror.

'I still don't look pretty, do I.'

Abe had to agree. 'You look like a regular bar room bruiser – *Zeke.*'

Ethan turned to him and patted his side.

'In that case we ought to do the job properly. A bruiser needs a sidearm. You said you could oblige?'

In answer Abe unlocked a bureau and took out a gunbelt with a Navy Colt .36. Ethan took it and buckled on the belt. Then he drew the gun, hefting it in his hand, listening to its action as he worked the hammer.

'Good balance and smooth action.' He slid it in and out of the holster, which he noted had been kept well and regularly treated. 'This tool has seen some action, I see,' he said.

Abe nodded with thin lips.

'It was a friend and a saviour to me once or twice,' he mused. 'Maybe it's seen too much action.'

Ethan slowly drew out half a dozen shells from the gunbelt and inserted them into the chamber. His lips were also drawn thin as he replied, 'And I reckon that maybe it still has work to do.'

Abe watched the way the younger man handled the weapon, aware that Ethan Grant was clearly no stranger to the use of a Navy Colt.

Despite Ethan's apparent outward calm he was desperate to see Laura, in order to see whether his voice would rouse her from the coma. Yet together, he and Abe agreed that it would be best not to rush over to Doc Tolson's, especially since they wanted to give some sense of versimilitude to Ethan's role as Zeke Kincaid. Accordingly, after Abe introduced 'Zeke' to the rest of the saloon staff, Ethan set about tuning the piano. Then he moved it so that it was strategically placed at the end of the long room opposite the bar, with a wall mirror in front of him so that he could see whatever was happening at the tables and in the main part of the saloon. Abe bustled about and drank a cup of coffee by the bar while Zeke practised. And indeed, he had to admit that though his repertoire was not extensive, his new piano-player was better than he had expected. With a nod of satisfaction he donned his hat and left.

Before long, possibly attracted by the long-absent strains of piano music, customers began filtering in. Nathaniel Grogan, the head barkeep, rejoiced in the increase in early morning trade, as did Flash Dan and the other semi-professional poker-players who ambled in and whose tables filled and emptied as successive groups of punters decided to try their hand against Lady Luck to the background accompaniment of Zeke Kincaid's quick-fingered repertoire.

Refusing all requests to join the punters for a drink, and acceding when he could to their requests for particular tunes, most of which he managed thanks to an ability to play by ear, Zeke kept up a steady flow of music.

By mid-morning Rufus took it upon himself to bring Zeke a man-sized glass of milk, which he left on the top of the piano.

'The boss shouldn't be too long at the Widow Cusworth's,' he said, wiping his hands on his apron as his foot automatically started tapping on the sawdust-covered floor. 'He's kind of like a beginner in the courting business,' he explained with that infectious smile of his that revealed good strong white teeth. 'Making money he can do, but he ain't no Don Juan.'

Zeke passed a few moments in jovial banter with the cook, mainly at Abe Gibson's expense, then Rufus left when Nathaniel dropped a hefty hint about chores that needed doing. Zeke looked in the mirror and watched him leave. And as he did so he became aware of a trio of men in range gear standing laughing at a corner of the bar. They had been washing trail dust off their tonsils with redeye for the better part of an hour, their banter and laughter getting all the time more raucous as their movements became more erratic. He saw that their attention had turned towards him. Then, as if they had reached some sort of agreement, they came swaggering towards him.

'Well, lookee here, a regular little milk-sop!' exclaimed one, seemingly the self-appointed chief heckler, a stocky, bristle-faced puncher with a lazy eye.

'Only he don't look like he's a regular piano-player,' said the second, a wiry-looking man of about Ethan's age. 'Look at his face, all cut and bruised. Maybe he's a fighting milk-sop'

Ethan played on, grinning into the mirror.

'You boys having a good time?'

'That's what we intended doing, milk-sop,' replied the first, now stationing himself on Ethan's left while the wiry fellow took up position behind him. 'Only we don't hold with the strangled-cat baloney you're knocking out of that box. Maybe you should give it a rest.'

Still Ethan played on, grinning affably.

'Maybe you boys have had enough to drink.'

The third member of the trio, a youngster barely accustomed to the razor, with penetrating, unblinking eyes piped up from Ethan's right.

'You saying we're drunk?'

'No sir,' replied Ethan. 'I'm just minding my business doing the entertaining job I'm paid to do.'

The lazy-eyed puncher growled.

'Well, we don't find you entertaining.'

'And we don't like looking at your battered face staring at us in the mirror, grinning like a monkey,' said the wiry cowpoke.

The youngster suddenly reached for the piano lid and slammed it down, barely missing Ethan's fingers. With the sudden bang and the end of the music the noise in the saloon subsided, only to be replaced by the scraping of chairs as the clientele sensed the onset of a drama that they wanted no part in. Ethan saw Nathaniel's reflection in the mirror and guessed that he was reaching towards a concealed weapon behind the bar. Ethan caught his eye and shook his head.

'Now why did you do that?' he asked.

'Because you ain't been showing us respect,' the stocky puncher volunteered.

'That so?' Ethan asked, nonchalantly picking up the glass of milk and sipping. Then suddenly he threw back his head and butted the wiry man in the pit of the stomach, at the same time flinging his milk in the face of the lazy-eyed puncher. The young man on his right immediately went for his gun, only to find Ethan's Navy Colt barrel jammed against his groin, the hammer ratcheted back. Ethan stood up, pushing the amazed youngster backwards, his hand still on the handle of his Peacemaker. The other two men seemed to sober up straight away, backing off a couple of paces with their hands in the air.

'Hey mister, we was just funning,' the youngster protested, with a sickly grin on his face.

'Oh?' Ethan replied. Then through clenched teeth: 'If I was you, boy, I'd raise my paws skywards – unless you want to risk your future matrimonial prospects.'

Nathaniel had come round the bar, a sawn-off shotgun in his brawny hands.

'Shuck those gunbelts now!' Ethan ordered as he lifted the glass he still held in his hand and drained the remains. He smacked his lips then smiled. 'Let me give you a piece of advice, boys. Give up strong drink and acquire a taste for milk. It's a lot . . . healthier!'

Nathaniel gathered up the three discarded gunbelts on his free arm and gestured with the shotgun towards the door.

'Now vamoose, you three. You can pick up your irons once you sober up. After that, don't expect any more service in this saloon. You're all barred.'

And, such being the way of the south-west, the crowd of onlookers who had backed away *en masse* from the potential trouble now advanced in a wave of ribald hilarity to watch the three disgraced punchers solemnly ejected through the bat-wing doors.

'Hey Zeke,' Nathaniel asked a few moments later as he returned to the bar. 'Where in hell did you learn to draw like that?' And the question was followed by a range of similar remarks and speculations from around the saloon.

'Fastest damned thing I ever saw.'

'Abe has got hisself a gunslinger.'

Already the local legend-weaving phenomenon was on the move. Even Rufus added his two-bits' worth, which was to have the biggest impact:

'I reckon he'd even make mincemeat out of Burt Lister.'

But Ethan didn't reply to Nathaniel for a few

moments. He was looking through the window, following a man riding down the street on a pony bearing the Rocking WB brand. It was Cole Burnett. He was surrounded by a group of street urchins who were gabbling away, offering to take care of his horse or to help him unsaddle.

'Nathaniel, I'm going to take a break for a spell. Figure I could do with a rest.' As he made his way through to the back of the saloon Ethan reflected that this was not the time to let Cole Burnett know that he was in Dirtville. He needed to think about why Cole had sent him to see a man with an envelope that contained nothing but blank paper.

SIX

Cole Burnett tossed some small change into the dirt and grinned as the urchins scrabbled about for it, like a flock of chickens after crumbs, then he dismounted and hitched his pony outside the sheriff's office. He mounted the steps and knocked curtly at the door, immediately letting himself in before hearing an answer. Mat Hughes was sitting with his feet on the desk, a quirly hanging from the corner of his mouth. On the other side of the desk his deputy, Burt Lister, was sitting with outstretched legs engrossed in his favoured activity of polishing his Remington .45.

'Sheriff Hughes?' Cole Burnett asked.

The lawman immediately snapped his feet down on the floor and ground his quirly out in an already overflowing ashtray.

'Yes sir, that's me. And you must be Mr Burnett.' They shook hands, then Cole Burnett looked hesitantly at the deputy, which seemed to prompt the sheriff. 'Burt, there seems to be more noise than usual this time of day from the Dead Ringer. Why don't you check it out.'

Realizing that this was not a request but an order, the deputy languidly rose, holstered his weapon and walked to the door. He tipped his hat at the newcomer then left. Cole watched him through the window as he strode across the street in the direction of the Dead Ringer saloon.

'Your deputy looks as if he could be handy to have around,' Cole remarked.

Mat Hughes snorted.

'Handy? Yeah, you could say that.' He gestured to the chair vacated by Burt Lister and crossed to the pot-bellied stove where a coffee-pot was kept permanently topped up. Selecting two cleanish mugs he poured a cup of Arbuckles for each of them, then sat back down behind his desk. 'Yup, he's handy all right,' he repeated. 'If it hadn't been for him the whole deal would have gone up in smoke. Now what are we going to do about it?'

On his way towards the Dead Ringer saloon Burt Lister was ambushed by three men.

'You've gotta do something, Deputy Lister,' said the first, the lazy-eyed *hombre* whose hair now hung lankly down the side of his face after his soaking with milk.

'Do something about what, Reardon?' the deputy queried cautiously. 'Just what in tarnation have you three gotten yourselves into? You're drunk as skunks.' He noted the absence of their sidearms, but made no comment about it.

The wiry individual, whose sobriquet given to him

by his fellows was 'Beanie' huffed indignantly.

'We washed away some dust, but we ain't drunk, deputy.'

'No, we was minding our own business when that cur of a piano-player assaulted us,' volunteered Dan Bannion, the youngest and most outraged of the trio. 'He shoved a gun in my groin and threatened me.'

The deputy's eyes narrowed. 'This piano-player, is he a newcomer?'

'Yessir,' replied Reardon. 'And he's still in there. He needs to be locked up or something.'

Burt Lister looked doubtfully at the three.

'Are you boys prepared to make a formal complaint, sign a statement?'

'That – that depends,' Beanie replied hesitatingly. 'On what?'

'On whether you figure you can take him in. He's about the fastest on the draw that I ever saw in my life.'

A strange look passed across the deputy's face, a mix of excitement and anger, as if a challenge had been delivered to him.

Then: 'If this feller needs arresting, then I'll arrest him all right. But I need proof that he's done something illegal, which means that I've gotta do some asking around.'

'You calling us liars?' growled Todd Reardon. Then he backed down quickly when he saw the deputy's jaw muscles tighten. 'I mean, you know us, Burt.'

Burt Lister grinned at the use of his Christian name, not because he liked the familiarity, but because he knew that a mere change in his facial expression was enough to frighten the bejeevers out of the likes of Todd Reardon and his cronies. The man was a bully, and like every bully he had ever met there was a point at which he would show his streak of yellow.

'Yeah, I know you, Reardon,' he replied. 'And I'm guessing you boys may have been trying to bully this guy, only he whopped you all.'

The three men cursed and protested, but Lister ignored them and strode past.

'I'll do a little investigating, like I said. Who knows, maybe this guy will want to press charges against you.' He allowed himself a smile of self-satisfaction as he heard them scurry away while he resumed his walk to the Dead Ringer saloon.

Abe had come back from Martha's Eatery in a state of high good humour. He had actually managed to give her a pretty good idea that he was attracted to her, and she had reciprocated. Reciprocated well enough to make him take her in his arms and kiss her good and hard. And she had melted in his arms, at least until some pain-in-the-ass customer had come knocking on the door in search of food.

The good humour evaporated as soon as Rufus and Nathaniel told him about the fracas between the three drunken punchers and his new piano-player, Zeke Kincaid.

'So where the hell is he now?' Abe asked, thumping a fist on the bar.

'Dunno, boss,' replied Nathaniel. 'He just said he

77

needed a rest. I ain't surprised after those three fools had given him trouble on his very first morning.'

'The damned fool! I'll have a word with him all right,' Abe murmured, more to himself than to Nathaniel. 'He's supposed to play piano, not tangle with riff-raff.'

Burt Lister's voice interrupted.

'I heard about that tangle you're talking about. I guess I better have a word with your piano-player myself. I've just had three shaken-up men accuse him of assaulting them.'

This information was met with a spontaneous eruption of invective and derision from several customers who had deliberately remained at the bar, within earshot of the deputy and the saloon-owner. To their number Nathaniel added his nickel's-worth.

'The drunken bums were looking for trouble and Zeke surely dished it out. I've got their gunbelts for when they sober up, but I told them not to come back after that. They got themselves barred.'

Abe gave his barkeeper a curt nod of approval.

'That's right, Lister. That's my house policy. A bad offence like that and they're barred until I say otherwise.'

The deputy took it all in and nodded.

'Looks like you're busier than usual for this time of the day.'

Rufus grinned. 'We got us a piano-player who knows a thing or two. Of course we're busy.'

'I think I'd like to meet this piano-player of yours,' the deputy mused. 'What's his name again?'

'Zeke Kincaid,' Abe replied. 'But he's not going to

cause any trouble, Lister. I'll make sure of that.'

Rufus guffawed. 'Well, boss, I reckon he could handle any trouble that comes along.' He looked challengingly at the deputy. 'I never saw anyone so fast!'

Abe saw that Rufus's jibe, intentional or not, had an effect upon Lister. It was like seeing a king rooster having his territory challenged by a young cockerel. He knew the signs. Feathers were likely to fly, and maybe blood as well.

'We'll see,' was all Lister said as he tipped his hat then turned and sauntered out.

'Blast it, Rufus! Why can't you learn to keep that jaw of yours closed,' Abe snapped. 'And that damn Zeke! Wherever he is.'

He hoped that he hadn't been fool enough to go visit Laura Hollister yet.

It had indeed been Ethan's intention to go to see Laura, but common sense had prevailed. Nonetheless, his encounter with the three cowpokes had left his nerves a tad frazzled and he realized that he had been near the point of doing something stupid. In a matter of a couple of days he had been sandbagged and left for dead, then informed that his precious Laura was lying in a coma after trying to shoot herself. And today he had taken on a new identity, been bullied by three drunken idiots and forced to draw on them. He could quite easily have squeezed the trigger. Indeed, part of him had wanted to pull the trigger to get rid of some anger.

And then Cole Burnett had arrived in Dirtville!

Why? Upon seeing him his hand had almost involuntarily reached for the handle of the Navy Colt and he realized that he had to get away. Which was why he found himself staring down at his 'own' grave in the town cemetery. It was a strange feeling. And for a second time he felt his hand reaching for his gun as he looked at the mound of earth under which lay the bastard who had put him through so much. It was at that point that he realized how Laura must have felt, for Abe had told him the whole story of how she had fired a shot into the ground before raising the derringer to her head.

The sound of the wrought-iron gate opening alerted a sixth sense and without waiting to see who had entered the cemetery he swiftly ran to gain cover behind the clapboard wall of the Dirtville church. He heard two voices, one of which made his hackles rise.

'You said he outdrew you?'

'You bet! Damn near crapped myself,' replied the sheriff. 'If it hadn't been for Lister that grave would be holding me.'

'Well, him being dead alters things a bit,' went on Cole Burnett, 'but we can allow for it. We just need to change our plans a bit.'

Ethan pressed himself against the wall of the church and clenched his fists tightly. He had an urge to jump out and confront the two men, maybe even goad them into going for their guns. But the logical side of him wanted to know why Walt Burnett, the finest man in the world, had died. Somehow Cole Burnett, whom Ethan had almost thought of as kin, was involved in something. And they were talking about plans! He pricked his ears up.

'I'll need the bags of gold back,' Cole Burnett said. 'I reckon Grover Wilkins will be impressed by them.'

'We'll stop by the office on our way,' replied the lawman. 'Do you still think he'll go for it?'

'He'll go for it all right. Now what about this woman who shot herself?'

Behind the church Ethan fought to keep his temper under control.

Just then a third voice intruded.

'I didn't expect to find you here, Sheriff.'

Mat Hughes sounded surprised. 'Burt, what the hell do you mean, sneaking up on me like that?'

Lister smirked. 'I was just doing what you always tell me to do, walking easy to get the element of surprise.'

'Not on me!' Hughes exclaimed. 'Mr Burnett here and I had some business to discuss.'

'Business that includes a dead man?' Lister asked suspiciously.

Neither of the other two replied for a moment, then Cole Burnett laughed.

'You're a sharp one, Deputy. That could get you a long way in life.'

'I hope so, Mr Burnett. I'm always looking for an opportunity to improve my position.'

Mat Hughes coughed. 'So what were you doing up here yourself?'

'Following a tip,' the deputy replied. 'Seems Abe Gibson has got himself a new piano-player.' He smirked again. 'The guy had only been working since this morning and already he's ruffled the feathers of a few of our local bully-boys. I thought I'd like to talk to him and I was told he'd been seen coming over in this direction. I guessed it was to see the town's latest attraction.'

'Well, there's only us here,' replied the sheriff.

'In that case, anything else you'd like me to do?'

Cole Burnett laughed his strange little hollow laugh.

'As a matter of fact, Deputy, there is.' And clapping Lister on the shoulder he gently guided him back down the path. 'There's something that the sheriff and I need to know.'

Ethan peeped round the side of the church when he heard the wrought-iron gate close. Then from behind him he heard a slight scuffle and a sound like a snigger. He spun round, his Navy Colt instantly out and poised.

'Don't shoot, *señor*!' gasped a youngster of about twelve dressed in ragged clothes that were at least a couple of sizes too large for him. By his side were a couple of similarly ragged boys a couple of years younger than him. Ethan suppressed a curse and holstered his weapon.

'Hey kids,' he said with a grin, 'don't ever sneak up on a man like that again.'

The three urchins shook their heads simultaneously, then the two younger ones took off.

'We didn't mean any harm, *señor*,' said the remaining boy, clearly the leader of the gang. 'We were just seeing if there was anything we could do to help you.'

Ethan warmed to the boy's genial cheeky expression, recognizing that he was hungry for any money

82

that he could scrape together. He fished in a pocket for a coin and held it out. He watched the grinning youngster make it disappear into a voluminous pocket, then he said with a wink:

'Information is always useful, son. You saw that man with the sheriff? Well I'd kinda like to know what he's doing in town. If you'd keep your eye on him and let me know if he does anything unusual or visits anyone special, I reckon I could make it worth your while.'

'It will be my pleasure, *señor*.'

'You can find me at the Dead Ringer,' Ethan said.

'I know, Mr Kincaid,' replied the boy. 'You're the new music-man.'

Ethan tousled his hair. 'Say, what's your name?'

'Vamoose, *señor*.' He grinned again. 'Everyone in Dirtville knows Vamoose. That's what they mostly shout at me!'

Grover Wilkins was in pain. Ever since he had lost his leg he experienced episodes of excruciating pain in the ankle of his artificial foot. People thought he was mad when he told them about it, which had really annoyed him when he was a youth. Then the War came along and hundreds of young men lost limbs, yet still complained of pain in their phantom limbs and he felt less of an outsider. Ordinarily a shot of rye would settle it, but when it got really bad he found that tobacco soaked in laudanum was the only half-decent cure. The only problem about it was that although no one except Doc Tolson knew that he took the drug, he was aware that it dulled his senses a mite. And that was why he tried to avoid taking it when he had any important business to conduct.

He was sitting in his big leather armchair in the study of his house on Main Street, with his artificial leg straight out on a footstool, smoking a large corn-cob pipe. His eyes were closed and his mind was floating in a sort of half-trance as the tobacco and the opium took the edge off his pain and lifted his spirits to a state of euphoria. He barely heard the tap on the door or the tread of boots across the wood floor.

'Hello, Uncle,' said Cole Burnett, coming in and gently tapping Grover Wilkins' artificial leg.

Grover Wilkins's eyes snapped open and he gulped laudanum-heavy smoke, which made him cough.

'Cole!' he exclaimed, laying the pipe in an ashtray and physically lifting his leg off the footstool. He leaned forward and gripped his nephew's outstretched hand. 'I'm sorry, boy. Walt didn't deserve to die like that. I'm sorry I couldn't make it to the funeral.'

Cole waved his hand dismissively.

'I didn't expect you to, Uncle Grover. Not with your leg and all. But it was a good, respectful funeral. I'm just glad that they shot the bastard that did it.'

Grover shook his head. 'I'd never have thought that boy could have done it. Not after Walt took him in and everything.'

Cole clenched his fists.

'Ethan Grant!' he grated. 'You didn't know him, Uncle Grover. He had a vicious side. I've just been to see his grave and I feel happy that my pa got justice.

84

I'm only sorry that it wasn't me that put him there, God rot his soul!'

Grover gestured towards the chair on the other side of the desk.

'So what brings you to Dirtville, Cole?'

The younger man raised his eyebrows in surprise. 'Don't you remember, Uncle? We had some business.'

It was Grover's turn to look surprised.

'Business? Now? Don't you think. . . ?'

'There's no better time,' Cole interrupted. 'It's what my pa would have wanted.' And from his vest pocket he produced a bag. 'Purest gold you're ever likely to see. All from the hills behind the Rocking WB. A lode that could make us as rich as Croesus. My pa staked a claim and we've been mining it, grinding it and preparing it with all the latest technology.'

Grover Wilkins opened the purse-string of the bag and let a little of the coarse gold-dust flow into the palm of his hand. At the sight of it he felt a little dizzy, although he was unsure whether it was the gold or the laudanum that made him feel thus. He had sufficient insight to realize that it was probably a combination of the two.

'What do you think, Uncle? Do you reckon you'd like to come in with us . . .' His face suddenly clouded with emotion and he hung his head. 'I mean – with me.' He seemed to recover himself. 'And I guess that's what my ma would have wanted, too.'

Grover Wilkins smiled as he let the gold-dust trickle from his hand back into the bag. He reached for his pipe and struck a light to it.

'I think maybe they would, Cole,' he replied, his eyes seeming to twinkle. 'But I'm a businessman. I think perhaps I need to come and take a look at your mine working.'

Cole grinned. 'That's just what I was hoping you'd say, Uncle.'

SEVEN

Red Cloud held the cup of the infused herbs, which her people called *ah-squah-na-to-quah,* and with a spoon let a trickle drop into Laura Hollister's mouth. She had searched out the corn-like wild herbs herself and found a small patch of them growing next to a stream inside the Pintos. Her father had shown her how to bruise the leaves and roots and prepare a decoction. It was a medicine with a great reputation for reviving wounded warriors and bringing them back from the jaws of death itself. Every hour of the day she had been dosing the pretty white woman, but as yet without effect.

The knock at the door was insistent. Red Cloud scowled. It irritated her that people would continue to call on the doctor even when he had left a note pinned to it saying that he was out visiting patients. She patted Laura's hand, silently willing her to come back to life where her young buck was waiting for her. The knocking started again and with a sigh she rose and went through. The town deputy was standing there. When he saw her a twisted smile played across his lips.

'Where's the doc?' he asked curtly.

Red Cloud shook her head and pointed to the note on the door.

Burt Lister leaned against the doorpost and hitched his thumbs in his gunbelt.

'You don't talk much, do you? What's your name again – Red Cloud, ain't it?' he grinned, displaying slightly crooked teeth.

Red Cloud made as if to close the door.

'Call later,' she said.

But Burt Lister casually stuck a foot in the door.

'My boss, the sheriff, wants some information,' he said, standing upright again and pushing the door open.

Red Cloud's eyes narrowed.

'Feisty thing, ain't you,' said Lister, reaching out and touching her cheek with a finger. 'You like white men, don't you? Maybe you'd like me as much as the doc.'

Red Cloud's eyes flashed anger and she brushed his hand away.

'Come later!' she repeated.

But again Lister merely grinned.

'I said I needed to know something. The doc's always so keen to get folks buried quickly, on account of the heat, so why hasn't that woman had her funeral yet.'

Red Cloud shook her head, her face expressionless.

Again Lister reached out, this time to put a hand on her shoulder.

'Maybe I'd better have a look at the body.' And with a shove he pushed her into the hall and then he stepped after her. 'Don't you even think about resisting the law,' he said sneeringly, reaching backwards with a foot to kick the door closed.

But before he could do so, the door was barged open. A hand caught him by the collar and he was yanked backwards.

'I don't know who you are,' came a voice, 'but I sure as hell don't like to see a man pushing a woman around.' And with a vicious tug Ethan ejected the deputy through the door, where he landed on his back in the dust.

Burt Lister's eyes registered first amazement, then fury. His hand shot to his side and closed over the handle of his Remington.

'Don't!' said Ethan. And to the deputy it seemed as if a gun had suddenly appeared in the hand of the derby-hatted individual in the gaudy vest who was confronting him. His gunhand froze.

'You've drawn against the law,' he snarled. 'I know you, mister. You're that new piano-player.'

Ethan shook his head, making no comment about his new job.

'I was just defending myself. You went for your gun first.'

Lister rose to his feet, staring angrily at the Navy Colt that was pointed unwaveringly at his chest.

'That's a lie.'

'Damn it, Lister, that was the truth,' came Abe Gibson's voice. 'I saw it. You went for your gun, then he drew.'

'And I saw it too,' said Doc Tolson. 'Just what do you want at my house, Deputy?'

Ethan holstered his weapon.

'I caught him harassing this lady.'

Lister was about to protest, when to his surprise he found himself pinned against the wall with the doctor's hand squeezing his throat.

'I took an oath to help people,' said Sam Tolson through grated teeth. 'But if you so much as even look disrespectful at Red Cloud again, I'll – make you wish you hadn't!'

A crowd of loafers had by this time gathered around the doctor's surgery, surprised to see the tableau that presented itself to their eyes. The deputy's face was turning purple. Red Cloud touched Sam Tolson's arm and as he looked at her face, the anger on his face seemed to dissolve. He released his grasp on the deputy's throat. 'Now get out of here before I press charges against you with the sheriff.'

Rubbing his throat, his mind seething with rage, Lister pushed his way through the crowd. He turned and glared when he heard a whistle and saw the boy called Vamoose grinning at the piano-player and making an imitation draw with an imaginary gun.

'Dammit!' Abe cursed. 'I'd say that the two of you have just seriously pissed off the deputy.' He sighed. 'And I reckon he's neither the forgetting nor forgiving type.'

Ethan sat beside the bed and gently clasped Laura's hand. He stroked her brow then leaned forward and brushed her lips with his.

'Laura – please wake up,' he whispered, pleadingly. 'I don't know how we've come to this, but I need you, darling.' He wiped tears from his eyes, then went on: 'If you can hear me, Laura, wake up soon.'

But she made no sign of awareness. She continued to breathe shallowly.

He continued watching her for a few moments, before hanging his head and involuntarily letting a sob escape. Then he felt a gentle hand squeeze his shoulder. He looked up and saw Red Cloud standing beside him with a mug of steaming coffee in her hand.

'She will come back,' she said, handing him the drink. 'When her spirit is strong enough she will come back from her dreamland.'

He nodded and watched her retreat noiselessly into the kitchen before he turned back to his fiancée.

'I'm praying Red Cloud is right, Laura,' he whispered. 'Because if she isn't, I'm going to have business to settle with the guy who put you here.' His mind conjured up a picture of Burt Lister, the man he had ejected unceremoniously from the doctor's house just a short while beforehand. So numbed had he been by everything that had happened, and so swiftly had events moved after Abe and the doc arrived, that he had only just realized that the deputy he had outdrawn was the same one who had goaded Laura at the cemetery. He unconsciously gritted his teeth as he thought of his missed opportunity, for he had had the deputy at his mercy. If anything happens to you, my darling, he thought to himself, I sure as

91

hell won't be so merciful again.

Sheriff Mat Hughes ground out a quirly in his ashtray, suppressing a smile as he listened to his deputy's account of his run-in with the piano-player, Zeke Kincaid.

'If'n that bastard hadn't winded me, he'd never have gotten the drop on me,' Lister said angrily, pacing up and down the office like a caged cougar.

'I think you need to calm down, Burt,' said Hughes at last. He looked from the deputy to Cole Burnett, who was sitting in a chair on the other side of the office, a cigar hanging languidly from between his lips. 'It looks like you were right, Cole,' he said. 'Doc Tolson has been holding out on the whole town for some reason. That woman who shot herself isn't dead.'

Burt Lister put a hand to his throat and rubbed. A couple of bruises had started to form on either side of his windpipe.

'I've got a score to settle with that damned horse-doctor, as well.'

Sheriff Hughes snorted. 'He's protective of that Navaho woman of his. You should have taken more care, Burt. Remember what I'm always telling you, never let anyone get behind you!'

The deputy's face became even more suffused with rage.

'I reckon I've got another score to settle there too, Sheriff.' He slammed his fist on the desk. 'And I mean to settle them all, real soon!'

Cole Burnett stood up and blew out a thin stream

of smoke from the side of his mouth. He grinned at the deputy, pulled out a thick wad of money and peeled off several bills.

'Burt, I think you found out just what we needed to know. Here's something for your trouble, so why don't you go and sink a few beers. It'd be good to help cool you down.'

The deputy accepted the money gratefully and left. As he did so, Mat Hughes struck a light to a fresh quirly, then volunteered:

'I can see why Burt's sore. That woman of the doc's is a real looker and Burt isn't the type to take kindly to being done down in front of a girl. He won't forgive easily.'

'And that could be just what we need,' replied Cole, tossing his cigar butt into the open door of the pot-bellied stove. 'In the meanwhile I guess that my uncle might be able to help where Burt left off.'

Abe felt like he was a kid again. Unseen magnets seemed to be drawing him to Martha's Eatery at the slightest opportunity. He sat drinking coffee while her last customers paid up and left, then he locked the door and turned the 'closed' sign to thwart any prospective newcomers. Then he went through to the kitchen where he found her waiting for him.

When the kissing stopped and they rose for air, Martha put her hands on his chest and gently pushed him out of whispering distance into regular conversation position.

'I hope that little girl makes it,' she said, wistfully.

Abe's brows furrowed.

'I hope so too, honey. If she doesn't I'm worried what Ethan will do. I don't place the lad as a killer, but the speed he has with a gun, one that ain't even his own, is powerful frightening. I reckon that he'd go looking for someone to blame.'

'And the first person would be Deputy Lister,' Martha agreed. She shivered and snuggled into his chest. 'I have a bad feeling, Abe. I feel we're heading for some sort of trouble in Dirtville.'

Sam Tolson was just showing his last patient out when he heard Grover Wilkins call to him from across the street. He looked over and saw the Dirtville entrepreneur limping in his direction. A younger man in smart range clothes was walking in step beside him.

'I thought it was about time that I collected some more of my mixture,' Grover announced.

Doc Tolson nodded. 'I have some ready and waiting, Grover. Come in.'

Once inside Grover introduced Cole Burnett.

'This is my nephew, Sam. That murderer Ethan Grant killed his pa, my brother-in-law, Walt Burnett.'

They shook hands.

'I'm truly sorry, Mr Burnett,' said Sam. 'Violent death is so cruel for the ones left behind.'

Cole sighed, the hint of tears forming in the corners of his eyes.

'I'm just glad the murderer got his deserts.' He bit his lip and added: 'I'm only sorry that it wasn't me that did it.'

Sam Tolson nodded, but made no comment. He crossed the room to a cabinet, unlocked it and drew out a brown bottle of liquid. He checked the label then handed it to Grover.

'I appreciate that, Sam,' said Grover, pocketing the bottle. He tapped his stick on the floor. 'To tell you the truth, Sam,' he went on, 'the word is that the woman who shot herself is still alive.'

Sam Tolson's face registered no emotion.

'Word gets around this town faster than the plague.' He nodded. 'Yes, the lady is still alive, but as to who she is, I have no idea and won't have until she recovers consciousness.'

'Then I reckon I need to see her,' said Cole firmly. 'I may be able to identify her. I hear that she claimed to be Ethan Grant's fiancée. Well, if she is, it's likely that I'd know her, or know her kin.'

'Ethan Grant was Walt Burnett's foreman,' Grover explained.

Sam Tolson considered for a moment, then:

'All right, Mr Burnett, I'll let you see her, but for a moment only. She's still in a coma and any shock could be fatal. But if she has relatives then you're right, we have to contact them.'

Red Cloud was sitting by the bed moistening the comatose woman's lips with her *ah-squah-na-ta-quah* potion, when the two men came in. Red Cloud immediately stood up and silently receded into a back room.

'My God! It's Laura Hollister!' gasped Cole Burnett. 'I was with Judge Hollister just yesterday and he said she'd been missing for a day. I – I never guessed that . . .' His face went pale and he looked genuinely pained as he looked at the heavy bandaging around her head. 'I think I better sit down,' he said, his knees looking as if they would buckle at any moment.

Sam and Grover helped him back into the consulting-room and sat him down in a large horsehair chair.

'Drink this, it will help,' said Sam, pouring a hefty measure of brandy and handing him the glass.

Cole downed it in one, relishing the restorative feeling that it gave him as it hit his stomach. He was actually feeling pretty pleased with himself over the little act he had just given. He had in fact half-expected to find Laura Hollister lying there, although it riled the hell out of him to think that she had preferred Ethan Grant to him. And with that thought his anger rose, fuelled by the hatred he already felt for the name of Ethan Grant, the man who he felt had well nigh ousted him in his father's affections.

Then his mind turned back to Laura Hollister. The bitch! he thought. He was suddenly glad to know that she was lying there half-dead. Then an unpleasant thought occurred to him.

'Are you all right now, Cole?' Grover Wilkins asked, concernedly.

Cole rubbed his brow and shook his head.

'I need to get out of here,' he mumbled. 'I need some air. Excuse me, gentlemen, I'll catch you later.' And he nodded and headed for the door.

When he had gone Grover turned to the doctor.

'I'm sorry about that, Sam, but I think they were close. It's shocked him.' He tapped his stick on the floor, then asked: 'Could she die, Sam?'

Sam Tolson pursed his lips and nodded. 'It's touch and go.'

'Then I guess we'd better let Judge Hollister know. The trouble is that the telegraph is down and Zach Holmes is out of town trying to fix it. Maybe I'd better let the sheriff know. I expect he'll send a rider over to Hagsworth.'

Mat Hughes was reluctantly going through his paper work when Cole Burnett let himself in. He threw his hat down on the sheriff's desk and slumped into a chair.

'I was right, it is Laura Hollister,' said Burnett. 'And she's in a bad way.'

'Then I guess I better send someone to let Judge Hollister know,' mused the sheriff.

'Maybe you had,' returned Cole Burnett, a sly smile spreading across his face. 'Only it might be an idea not to rush.'

'Meaning?'

'That we don't want a judge nosing around here before we're ready.'

The sheriff let out a short conspiratorial laugh, then opened a drawer of his desk.

'If you'd like to pass a couple of mugs, Cole,' he said, uncorking a bottle of whiskey, 'I reckon we should have a little drink to the future. The way I see it, the future sure looks rosy.'

EIGHT

Martha's Eatery was inevitably busy at six o'clock as people, especially single men, opted for a wholesome cooked meal in congenial surroundings instead of hastily prepared grub cooked by themselves after a long day's toil. Apart from which, Martha knew how to stimulate the stomach juices of passers-by, always having coffee percolating near the open kitchen window, together with a slowly simmering skillet full of butter, herbs and a few chunks of meat. The contents of this skillet were never for actual consumption, since she was fully confident in her ability to whip up any of the meals on her menu – from antelope stew to T-bone steaks followed by blue-berry pie – yet it did the trick. Her eatery was always the busiest in Dirtville.

Abe Gibson watched admiringly as Martha bobbed between tables, serving food skilfully and efficiently, for apart from a single kitchen-girl-cum-waitress she did all of the work herself. He was roused from his reverie by a remark of Ethan's.

'S . . . sorry, Ethan, what was that again?'

'I said, love is blind, Abe. A man could ask you for your wallet when Martha is nearby and you'd hand it over before the question registered in your brain. You've got it bad, I reckon.'

Abe straightened his cutlery and nodded.

'Reckon I have – *Zeke*! But I'm thinking that so do you.'

Ethan bit his lip. 'Only I'm watching the woman I love hover on a knife-edge.'

Abe Gibson frowned, sympathetically.

'I know, son. But she's going to pull through. I know she will. Doc Tolson is one smart doctor.' He looked up and beamed as Martha approached with two piping-hot plates of stew. 'You would agree with that, wouldn't you, honey. Doc Tolson is one smart doctor.'

He leaned over the table and added emphatically; 'I'm trying to tell Zeke here that he'll get Laura better.'

Martha set the plates down and replied in a low voice.

'Of course, he's about the best doctor we've ever had in Dirtville. But don't forget about Red Cloud. She's doing her best with her people's medicine. I've seen how well some of her herbs work with our ladies after they've given birth. And Sam Tolson is sensible enough to realize the importance of some of these natural medicines.'

Ethan nodded approvingly and replied in an equally low voice.

'Just whatever it takes, Martha. If Red Cloud gets my Laura back to consciousness then I'll give her the shirt off my back.'

'You mean you'll give her my shirt off your back,' put in Abe with a grin.

Martha gave him a mock cuff on the shoulder, then left to tend to her other customers while the two men got on with their meal. So engrossed were they with sating their gastric juices, and with their conversation about Laura, that they were hardly aware of the tinkly bell on the door which alerted Martha that another customer had just come in.

'Evening, Abe,' said Sheriff Hughes. 'Are you going to introduce me to your friend?'

Abe looked up, with his fork half-way to his mouth, then, somewhat nonplussed, replied:

'Sure thing, Mat. This is Zeke Kincaid, my new piano-player.'

Ethan swallowed a mouthful of stew and held out his hand.

'My ma always taught me to be respectful of the law,' he said with a grin. 'Howdy, Sheriff.'

Mat Hughes' smile did not accord with the look in his eyes. He shook hands.

'Respect for the law is important, mister piano-player,' he said. 'I understand that you had a run-in with my deputy.'

Ethan took a sip of water before shaking his head.

'No run-in as far as I'm concerned, I just ejected a jasper from the doctor's place. He seemed to be bothering the doctor's wife.'

'The doctor's woman, you mean,' Mat Hughes corrected. 'As far as I know, they ain't legally wed. But that's another matter. I heard that you drew a gun on my deputy. Drawing a gun against an officer of the law is a run-in in my book. And I'm taking it seriously.'

'Now lookee here, Sheriff,' began Abe, but Ethan gave him a gentle kick to silence him.

Ethan had continued to eat nonchalantly, his regard seemingly focused on his food. But now he laid down his fork and clicked his tongue.

'Is that so, Sheriff? Well, if I were you I reckon I'd consider what sort of a deputy I'd want to help me.' His eyes suddenly shot up, staring at the sheriff eyeball to eyeball. 'In my book a man doesn't harass a woman.'

Veins seemed to have stood out on Mat Hughes' temple. He forced a smile.

'I wasn't inferring anything,' he said. He tapped his star. 'Only I'd appreciate it if you didn't go pointing that gun at an officer of the law again. That would upset me a great deal.'

Ethan said nothing for a moment as he considered the sheriff's words. Then he reached forward and plucked a toothpick from the little jar in the centre of the table, and applied it to his teeth.

'And I'd appreciate it, Sheriff, if you'd stick to just minding the law. I've not broken any statute or local ordinance, but I take rare exception to anyone who steps over the boundaries of accepted decency. Your deputy did that with the doctor's wife, just as I hear he did with that young woman who shot herself.'

Abe silently groaned, but said nothing. There was nothing for it but for him to watch Ethan play out his game.

'That ain't true,' growled the sheriff. 'Besides, it's got nothing to do with what we're talking about.'

Ethan suddenly stood up and stepped round the table to within a pace of the sheriff.

'I disagree, Sheriff,' he said. 'And as for pointing my gun at anyone – I'll decide whether it's appropriate or not.' A grin spread across his face. 'Of course, if you'd like to take this gun off me, that's a different matter.' The smile faded suddenly. 'But just be aware that I'm kinda attached to this gun.'

Sheriff Hughes returned the stare for a moment, then he nodded his head.

'I'll let you keep your gun, for now. But I'm going to be watching you, Zeke Kincaid.' He took a backward step towards the door. Just then Martha came out of the kitchen and bumped into him, only just avoiding spilling the coffee-pot in her hand.

'Why, Sheriff Hughes,' she said with a hesitant smile as she took in Ethan's stance by the table upon which lay his half-eaten meal. 'Is there anything wrong?'

The sheriff gave Ethan a final withering look, before turning to Martha with a smile.

'Nothing at the moment, ma'am. I was just checking on the sort of clientele that you're getting.' And then tipping his hat he looked at both Ethan and Abe. 'Gentlemen, just remember what I said. I'll be watching.'

Burt Lister had been drinking for three hours in one of the dirt-floored drinking-holes on the outskirts of the town. His black mood had not brightened despite the attentions of one of the house whores or the bottle of tequila that he had drained. Indeed, if anything his hatred for the man who had humiliated him earlier had been fuelled tenfold.

Mat Hughes found him and took him for a walk in the moonlight, before steering him back to the office for a few strong mugs of wake-up coffee.

'What are you playing at, Burt?' he demanded when, at last, his deputy's eyes seemed to be focusing properly upon him. 'Mr Burnett gave you some dough to lighten up, not to get blind drunk!'

'What's the matter, Sheriff,' Lister replied sneeringly. 'You got some sort of special work for me to do?'

Sheriff Hughes struck a light to a quirly and blew smoke ceilingwards. He picked a speck of loose tobacco from his lip and flicked it away.

'I have, as a matter of fact. That piano-player needs bringing down a peg.'

A grin spread across the deputy's face.

'Are you gonna take his gun off him?' he asked sarcastically.

Hughes shook his head.

'No Burt, I'm not.' He flicked ash into the brimming ashtray and grinned maliciously, then: 'You are.'

Lister raised his eyebrows and opened his mouth to reply, but the sheriff cut him off.

'I reckon we'll play the game the same way we did with that Ethan Grant feller. The only difference this time will be the fact that you'll be the one who faces him. I'll be there ready, just in case.'

Lister chuckled. 'You won't be needed, Sheriff.' The grin faded from his face. 'This time I'm gonna make that bastard sorry he was ever born – if he lives long enough to have any such thought.'

Sheriff Hughes blew out a thin stream of smoke, then ground his quirly in the ashtray. He contemplated it for a moment, as if emptying it was a chore that he hated doing, then he tipped the contents into the stove.

'We'll do it later on. So right now I want you to go home and get a little shut-eye. I'll rouse you when the time is right.'

Once he had gone, Cole Burnett came in from the cells, where he had been sitting and listening.

'You did just fine there, Mat.' He struck a light to a cigar and tossed the match into the empty ashtray, then observed: 'I see you've been doing a little house-cleaning. That's good. We want everything to be tidy and clean, don't we.'

They both laughed as Hughes opened the whiskey drawer.

Ethan and Abe had gone from Martha's Eatery to Doc Tolson's, where they sat with Laura for a little over an hour. During that time Ethan had more or less kept up a continuous monologue, punctuated at times by questions addressed to Laura. But each time that the comatose woman failed to register awareness, he swept on with the monologue. Abe watched, aware that the younger man was eating his heart out.

On the way back to the Dead Ringer Abe asked:

'Why did you mention anything to the sheriff

about Laura shooting herself and being goaded by the deputy?'

'I wanted to see his reaction,' Ethan replied. 'That and the fact that I didn't like him.'

'Mat Hughes has done a good enough job for Dirtville and kept the peace pretty well,' Abe protested. 'I guess it's no secret that he answers to Grover Wilkins, but that's no different from most towns in this part of the world. The biggest wheel usually has the local lawman running along with him.'

'And how do you know that Grover Wilkins is straight?'

'Who knows how straight any man is?' Abe replied.

'Exactly!' said Ethan.

They had reached the Dead Ringer and pushed open the batwing door. Abe shook his head and stopped Ethan on the threshold.

'Why is it that I get the impression that trouble follows you – Zeke?' Then, before the other could reply, he pointed at the piano and the gathering crowd by the bar. He raised his voice more than was strictly necessary, as if moving into impresario mode. 'Now how about you give the paying customers a little music, and earn some of the money I'm paying you!'

Ethan grinned and replied, equally loudly:

'Money? Well, boss, that sure is the first time you've ever mentioned money.'

Nathaniel Grogan's voice came over the heads of the drinking crowd.

'Watch out, Zeke. Boss is good about talking money, but showing it is another matter.'

*

Grover Wilkins puffed his pipe alight, savouring the dark tobacco, despite its being devoid of laudanum since his nephew was present. With a glass of his best rye whiskey in his hand he was enjoying himself and felt no pain whatever from his phantom limb.

'Uncle Grover, this mine is going to solve all the problems about the ranch and make us a fortune into the bargain.'

Grover smoked contentedly and nodded.

'Cole, I guess you could say that I've been fortunate enough to have amassed a fortune already. The truth is though, that at my time of life what matters most is knowing that you got it right.'

'Then here's to tomorrow and to getting it right, Uncle,' said Cole with a laugh, as he raised his own glass.

'Amen to that,' replied Grover, draining his glass in one. 'To tomorrow.'

Vamoose's eyes gleamed as he watched the man toss the silver dollar up and down in his hand.

'So you'll tell him it's an emergency,' the man instructed. 'He's to come straight away, because there is blood all over the place.'

The urchin grinned, displaying his lopsided teeth.

'I will tell him, *señor.*'

'And who will you say sent you?'

'Mr Holmes, the telegraph man.'

'And you won't mention me!'

Vamoose feigned surprise. 'I've never seen you

before, *señor.*'

The coin was flicked into a graceful parabolic arc and deftly caught and vanished by the boy.

'You're a good kid,' said the man, tousling his hair.

The Dead Ringer was lit up by half a dozen kerosene-lanterns, each surrounded by an arrangement of chandelier-like cut glass, which Abe Gibson had imported from New Orleans to give the saloon what he believed to be a touch of class. The gaming-tables were in full swing and Nathaniel and the other barkeepers were rushed off their feet as they dispensed beer and whiskey to the paying clientele. Zeke sat on his stool, a glass of milk on the piano, while he beat out a lively ditty that sounded as if it had come from Mexico.

Nathaniel, ever watchful as a good bartender should be, saw the batwing doors open and Vamoose creep in.

'Hey you,' he shouted. 'Vamoose!'

But the boy just grinned and pointed at Ethan. Before Nathaniel could do anything he had weaved a way through the crowd towards the piano-player. Ethan turned when he felt the boy tug his sleeve. He smiled and leaned closer as the urchin cupped a hand to his mouth and whispered in his ear. Then he nodded, fmished his tune and stood up. He signalled to Nathaniel that he was taking a five-minute break.

Vamoose was waiting by the door and dashed out into the darkness as Ethan followed.

When Ethan returned ten minutes later he merely shrugged in reply to Nathaniel's enquiry as to what the boy wanted.

'Where's the boss? Ethan asked.

'At Martha's Eatery, where else,' volunteered Rufus, the cook, who was enjoying a couple of beers with rye chasers before turning in.

'He won't be back before throwing-out time, I reckon,' added Nathaniel, taking time out to swallow a mouthful of beer.

Ethan exchanged good-natured banter with them before resuming his stool and starting to play again.

After a few moments Rufus swivelled round on his barstool.

'Uh oh!' he exclaimed under his breath. He tapped the counter to attract Nathaniel's attention.

'I thought you told that jasper to stay away from here,' he said.

Nathaniel was just applying a match to a cheroot. He looked up and followed Rufus's pointing finger to see Todd Reardon enter with Deputy Burt Lister.

'This could mean trouble, Rufus,' he whispered. 'Maybe you best go and get the boss.'

Rufus looked hesitantly at his drink, then gulped it back before sliding off his barstool and making his way towards the back door. Nathaniel meanwhile chewed the end of his cheroot, manoeuvring it into a comfortable position in the corner of his mouth.

'What can I do for you, Deputy?' he asked, wiping the bartop in front of Lister. '*You*'re welcome,' he went on, removing his cigar and jabbing it in Reardon's direction. 'But as I guess you know, this jasper isn't. He's been barred.'

'He's with me,' replied Lister nonchalantly. Then: 'We'll have a couple of shots.' He turned to face the interior of the saloon and leaned back against the bar, supporting himself on his elbows.

'That's him!' said Reardon loudly, pointing extravagantly at Zeke the piano-player. 'He's the bastard that abused me and my buddies.'

The volume of the accusation was not without effect. People along the bar went silent, and like a wave of expectation the general chatter and clatter in the saloon subsided. Only the music from the piano continued.

Burt Lister reached for his whiskey and downed it in one swallow.

'You sure about that, Reardon?'

'It's him all right.'

Burt Lister nodded, then heaved himself away from the bar. He adjusted his gunbelt as he moved towards the piano-player, who seemed oblivious to it all.

Nathaniel chewed nervously on his cigar. Then he saw the batwing-doors slowly open and he began to heave a sigh of relief, expecting it to be Rufus returning with Abe. But then he saw Sheriff Hughes silently enter and immediately turn left, as if to circle the room. His heart began to race, for he had seen a similar move a few days ago.

The night that Ethan Grant had been shot in the back of the head.

NINE

Despite his nonchalance Ethan had missed nothing. With his derby hat tipped at an angle to shade his eyes, he had kept a watch on the reflections in the mirror. He recognized Reardon and the deputy, and he had seen the sheriff sidle in and circle the back of the saloon to take up a position behind him. Lister and Reardon were walking in his direction when he suddenly stopped playing the old Mexican ditty he'd been banging out and instead began playing 'Three Blind Mice' with some exaggeration.

The sudden change brought a few howls of laughter from the customers at the bar. Ethan then slammed the piano lid down and spun round on his stool to face Lister.

'Is there some reason for you to sneak up on me, Deputy?' he demanded.

Burt Lister had stopped in his tracks at the first sound of laughter, his hackles prickling at the thought that folks might be laughing at him. He felt his face flush and he scowled.

'I'm looking for you, all right.'

An innocent smile flashed across Ethan's face.

'Well, you've found me, I guess. Zeke Kincaid, the piano-player is right here playing the piano, at your service.'

A few guffaws from the bar helped to inflame the deputy's temper.

Then the smile suddenly vanished from Ethan's countenance as he fixed on Reardon.

'But why have you brought this scum. He was thrown out yesterday and told never to come back.'

Reardon sneered. 'Looks like the boot's on the other foot now. Soon you'll—'

'I'll handle this, Reardon!' Lister snapped. Then to Ethan:

'This man claims you abused him.'

Ethan shook his head.

'I gave him and his two partners a lesson about not playing with guns.'

A sly grin hovered over Lister's lips.

'So you threatened them?'

Ethan folded his arms and shook his head again.

'Nope, I warned them, that's all. There's a difference, you see. I'm always prepared to give a warning – once! So if I were you, Deputy, I'd back off.'

A muscle in Lister's jaw tightened.

'You threatening me now, pilgrim?'

'I just told you, I don't threaten, but I warn folk.' His eyes narrowed beneath the rim of his derby. 'So don't do anything sudden, Lister.' Then he raised his voice. 'And that goes for you too, Sheriff. You see, I kinda take exception to men trying to sandbag me!'

Lister's hand twitched above his gun.

111

'You dirty ratbag, I've a mind to—'

'Don't move, Burt!' barked Mat Hughes, stepping forward to stand in front of Ethan. 'And now, mister smart-ass piano-player, I'll trouble you for your gun.'

Ethan smirked, then shook his head.

'Like I told you earlier, Sheriff, I'm attached to my gun and *no one* takes it off me without a real good reason.'

'I'll give him reason, Sheriff,' Lister snarled. 'If he wants to chance his luck.'

Sheriff Hughes raised a hand.

'You'll do nothing, Burt.' He held out his hand towards Ethan. 'I said, I'll trouble you for that gun. I'm taking it for safe-keeping.'

Ethan's face was deadpan.

'Without a real reason, you can go to hell.'

Nathaniel lifted the sawn-off shotgun that he kept behind the bar and patted its stock emphatically.

'Zeke's right, Sheriff. You've got no cause to ask for his weapon. He didn't do anything to Reardon and his two cronies that they didn't deserve. Why don't you just go and arrest someone for some real crime.' And the glare that he gave Reardon caused the cowpoke to take a step backwards into the relative safety of the crowd at the bar.

Sensing an impasse, Sheriff Hughes nodded to his deputy.

'Come on, Burt. Maybe Nathaniel has a point. Let's go do our evening round of the town.'

But the young deputy was in no mood to leave. He had already been bested once by the derby-hatted piano-player. His fingers hovered over the gun butt.

Ethan was still sitting with his arms folded.

'I agree with Nathaniel, Sheriff. You ought to go and arrest some real criminal. I hear you've got a woman-molester in town!'

Burt Lister's eyes positively flared with anger. His hand darted to his gun and he drew.

There was the explosion of a single shot and the gun fell from Lister's hand as a bullet bored through the muscles of his upper arm and spun him round to collapse against the bar. Sheriff Hughes had immediately gone for his gun, only to halt in mid-draw as the hammer of Ethan's weapon was ratcheted back, ready to send instant death his way.

'How did you like it, Deputy?' Ethan demanded, his face white with pent-up fury. 'I hear that's what you did to a woman a few days back. You goaded her – and she shot herself!' He stepped closer to the bleeding deputy, whose face registered nothing but pure hatred. 'I reckon you'd best get him to a doctor, Sheriff,' said Ethan, holstering his weapon.

Suddenly, the batwing-doors were thrust open and Abe and Rufus rushed in. The crowd, which had just begun to murmur after the shock of the violent confrontation that had taken place, went silent again when they saw the look of horror written across Abe Gibson's face. He seemed to have no curiosity about the tableau that presented itself in his saloon. Instead, he blurted out:

'Sheriff! You've gotta come. Doc Tolson – he's dead. His . . . his—'

Rufus finished the sentence for him. 'His throat's been cut!'

*

It seemed as if everyone in the saloon had followed Abe and the Sheriff outside. Some thinking *hombres* produced kerosene-lamps from somewhere and a few moments later the alley was crammed with people eager to see the grisly sight illumined by lamplight.

Doc Sam Tolson lay on his side, his eyes wide open and sightless, one arm buckled under him and the other outstretched towards his medical bag, which lay a few feet away as if in his dying moment it had been flung from his hand. An expanding pool of blood was soaking into the dirt from an ugly gaping wound in his neck. Mat Hughes knelt down and felt for a pulse in his neck, knowing full well that it was a futile gesture, for form's sake.

'He's dead, all right,' he said, straightening up and looking about him. 'Anybody see a knife?'

A murmur rose from the gathered crowd, which seemed to rise into a chorus of amazement, horror and anger. Then the near hysterical mumblings began.

'What sort of bastard would kill a doctor?'

'If they killed the doc, then no one's safe!'

'What you gonna do, Sheriff?'

Mat Hughes sensed the growing mood of the crowd and knew from past experience how such a half-liquored gathering could become a frenzied mob capable of ripping a town apart. He raised his arms and called for quiet, then, when that didn't work, he drew his gun and fired once into the air.

Silence descended instantaneously.

'The law will handle this,' he cried. 'Now all of you, clear out and go quietly about your business. I need to examine the area, then me and—' He stopped, suddenly recalling that his deputy had just been wounded and was himself in need of medical attention. But now the town was without a doctor.

'I'm here, Sheriff,' came Burt Lister's voice. The deputy pushed his way through the already departing crowd. 'It was just a flesh wound,' he said, flicking his eyes at the bloodstained bandanna he had tied about his upper arm. 'Are we gonna arrest him?' he asked, pointing at Ethan.

Ethan was standing beside Abe, both of them looking shocked at the discovery of the doctor's body.

'No one's arresting me for anything, Lister,' Ethan returned. 'You drew on me. You're lucky I decided to let you live.'

The deputy's face went puce in the moonlight.

'You mangy dog. Why for two pins, I'd—'

'You'll calm down, Burt!' barked Sheriff Hughes. 'We've got a murder here. The town doctor was a good man, and he's been butchered while we've been squabbling. Now we've got a job to do.'

Abe touched the sheriff's arm.

'We'll have to move the body someplace,' he said, shaking his head with pursed lips. Sheriff Hughes understood. Ordinarily a dead body would be taken to Doc Tolson's, but that was out of the question now.

'Dammit!' Hughes exclaimed. 'Somebody will have to tell his woman.'

Ethan pulled Abe's sleeve.

'Let's go tell her,' he said. 'His wife has a right to know that her husband won't be coming home any more.'

He knew that no one would miss the urchin. Finding him afterwards had been easy, as had luring him behind the courthouse with the promise of another silver dollar. But Vamoose did not realize that the flash of silver that he saw in the moonlight was not from a silver dollar, but from the blade of a knife. He only began to panic as the hand was clapped over his mouth and his head was bent backwards. By the time the knife raked across his throat, it was too late.

Abe and Ethan were grateful that Martha had come to investigate the noise, since neither of them relished the prospect of telling Red Cloud about Sam's murder. A woman's presence made them feel less uncomfortable. But as it was, Red Cloud seemed to have sensed the tragedy that they were about to impart before any of the three spoke. She had just left Laura Hollister after administering a little of her *ah-squah-na-ta-quah* potion, and was boiling up a pot of coffee on the stove in readiness for Sam Tolson's return from the emergency visit he had been called away on.

'He is dead?' she asked.

Martha's eyes were moist and she bore an expression of immense sadness. 'I am so sorry, Red Cloud.'

'He has been killed?'

The two men stood with bent, embarrassed heads and let Martha explain.

'He was murdered, killed with a knife.' She held out her arms to embrace the doctor's widow, but Red Cloud held out a hand, her face expressionless. She shook her head.

'I must finish his work,' she said, turning and going back into the room where Laura Hollister lay unconscious, oblivious to the tragedy that had befallen her nurse.

Martha whispered to Ethan and Abe, 'You two go. I'll stay with her. She's in shock and it might just suddenly hit her.'

Abe nodded and gestured for Ethan to follow him. He at least felt badly in need of a drink.

Mat Hughes knocked on the door about an hour later and was answered by Martha.

'I realize the news must have got here, Martha,' he said. 'That must be why you're here, right? You're looking after the doc's woman.'

Martha eyed him scornfully.

'Red Cloud is the doctor's *wife*,' she corrected. Then she frowned and lowered her tone. 'I mean, his widow!'

The sheriff stood with his thumbs tucked into his gunbelt. 'She must be in a hell of a state. Not able to talk, I guess.'

'She's upset, of course.'

The sheriff nodded. 'Which of course is why we didn't bring – er – the body over here, like we normally would. I suppose I'd better try and find someone else to – embalm him.'

'I will attend to my husband's body,' came Red

117

Cloud's voice from the door of the bedroom. 'Please have him brought here.'

Hughes stared at her for a moment, then tipped his hat.

'It seems sort of irregular, but if that's what you want, I'll have some boys bring his body over from the jail.'

Martha was about to close the door, but the sheriff coughed then went on:

'Actually there is another matter. The woman – Laura Hollister – we've got to consider what to do about her. I've sent a rider to Hagsworth, but whether or not he's gotten hold of the judge I don't know. But one thing is certain, I need to make sure that she's receiving the best possible care.' He shuffled his feet with an embarrassed air. 'Now that the doc is dead, I guess the best thing would be to move her to the Dirtville Hotel. Grover Wilkins has said that we can use one of the rooms and he'll waive any bill. Seems a generous offer.'

Red Cloud was standing with her arms folded. She shook her head.

'I must look after her. If she is moved, she might die.'

'But she ain't a doctor,' Hughes said, talking to Martha. 'Besides, she needs her own people to look after her.'

Martha felt her ire rise.

'She has got her own people looking after her,' she replied icily. 'Women! Two of us. I'm staying here to help Red Cloud.'

The sheriff looked unsure. 'Maybe I better ask Sol

Arthur, the blacksmith, to call by. He knows a lot about horse-doctoring.'

Martha began to close the door. 'We will look after her, Sheriff And we don't need the help of a black-smith!'

Mat Hughes stood looking at the closed door, a slow smile spreading across his face.

Later on, after he had overseen the removal of the doctor's body to his surgery, Sheriff Hughes did pay a visit to Sol Arthur, the blacksmith. And he took Burt Lister with him, and watched as the blacksmith cauterized the deputy's arm to stanch the loss of any more blood. He couldn't afford to have the deputy lose his strength. After all, there was still work planned for him.

It was almost midnight by the time he sat down in his office, with a last mug of coffee beside him and a fresh quirly hanging from his lips, as he prepared to write a report of the evening's events. He was inter-rupted by a furious knocking on the door, then by its being thrust open to reveal a couple of the town loafers, wide-eyed and ashen pale.

'Sheriff! There's been another murder,' one blurted out. 'It's that kid, Vamoose. He's been throat-cut as well!'

TEN

Abe Gibson felt sick when he heard about the slaying of Vamoose. Together with Ethan he volunteered to take the body of the boy to Doc Tolson's surgery, for he was sure that Red Cloud would be willing to prepare his body. He was aware that the Navaho woman had been kinder to Vamoose and his gang of fellow-urchins than most of the Dirtville citizens. And sure enough, Red Cloud told them where to lay his body in the back room, on a deal table next to the body of Sam Tolson. Barely a sign of emotion did she display, until she was alone with the two bodies, behind the closed door.

Her screaming was the strangest thing that he'd ever heard. Not so much an agonized scream of anguish, but a controlled scream-cum-yell of woe. A look at Ethan's face told him that he had formed the same opinion.

'It's her people's way,' Martha said. 'She's letting her pain out first, so that she can get on with whatever she has to do.'

And indeed, for ten minutes or so Red Cloud

carried on with her wailing, which as it went on became more recognizable as a rhythmic dirge. Then abruptly it stopped. After about an hour Ethan ventured to tap on the door and push it open a few inches.

'They are almost ready,' Red Cloud said, without turning to face him. She was washing her hands in the far corner of the room. On the two tables lay the bodies of Sam Tolson and Vamoose, both cleaned and laid out in shrouds, their awful wounds stanched and concealed, so that they looked as if they had merely fallen asleep.

'They look beautiful, Red Cloud,' he half-whispered. 'Whoever did this will get what's coming to them.'

The Navaho woman turned, her beautiful black eyes fixing his for a moment. Then she shook her head and walked past him.

'I must see to your Laura now.'

Martha had been sitting with Laura while Abe drank coffee. As Red Cloud relieved her she put a hand on her wrist.

'You don't have to do this, Red Cloud. You look exhausted. I'll sit with her tonight.'

But already the town doctor's widow was going through the checks that her husband had shown her. She pulled up the unconscious woman's eyelids one at a time and inspected her pupils, then she put an ear to her chest and listened to her heart. When she straightened up, concern was written across her face.

'She is getting weaker. I will sit with her. You sleep.'

Martha acquiesced reluctantly and went through

to join Abe and Ethan at the kitchen table where they were drinking strong black coffee.

'Just who the hell could do something like this?' Abe sighed. 'To kill a man like Sam Tolson in cold blood.'

'And that poor little boy, Vamoose!' gasped Martha. 'What motive could they have?'

'It's the work of a lunatic,' Abe growled, pouring Martha a coffee.

Ethan shook his head. 'That was no lunatic's work. Whoever killed them both knew exactly what they were doing.'

Abe and Martha both shot him looks of astonishment.

'Well think about it,' Ethan went on. 'Why would anyone kill the doc?'

Abe snapped his fingers. 'Red Cloud! It could be because someone has designs on her, and Sam was in the way.'

Martha nodded, her eyes wide with disbelief.

'Someone like Burt Lister, you mean?'

Ethan raised a finger to his lips and pointed to the bedroom door.

'Actually, no. That's a possibility, but I don't think so. I'm wondering if it has more to do with Laura.'

'My God, Ethan, you don't think . . .' began Martha, with a gasp.

Ethan swallowed a mouthful of coffee.

'That's exactly what I think. Someone is trying to make sure that Laura doesn't make it. Killing the doc would be a way of achieving that.'

'And what about Vamoose? Why kill him?'

Ethan stroked his chin. 'That doesn't figure. And that really worries me.'

The noise of raised voices and angry drunken mumblings from outside had been getting gradually louder. Martha shivered, then: 'One thing is sure,' she said. 'These murders have wakened the ugly side of Dirtville.'

The mood of Dirtville did not improve the next morning. Fear, indignation and pure stark horror seemed to have motivated the citizens to rise early with the dawn. Everyone seemed up in arms, scouring the area of the two murder scenes. Some came out of sheer ghoulish curiosity, others out of a genuine desire to help. Ironically, it fell to a couple of the town urchins to supply the clue that had evaded the searchers of the previous evening.

Sheriff Hughes had breakfasted early and set to work straight away. A killing always meant that he'd be busy as folk tended to ally themselves with the law, while at the same time heaping expectation upon the sheriff to put the killer behind bars as soon as possible. The problem with these deaths, of course, was the fact that there was no obvious suspect to go after, to arrest and put behind bars.

Grover Wilkins was not the least vociferous of the visitors to Mat Hughes' office that morning. 'We need a quick result, Hughes! And we've gotta get a new town doctor. How's the telegraph situation?'

Sheriff Hughes sometimes intensely resented the attitude of the town's entrepreneur, but he swallowed his pride and answered calmly.

'Still waiting for Zach Holmes to get back to us. If I don't hear from him today, I'll send another man to Hagsworth. I already sent one to let the judge know about his daughter.'

'Wel, I'll have to leave it to you,' Grover went on. 'I'm going to be away on business for a few days with my nephew, Cole Burnett.'

Mat Hughes watched him hobble across the street to check on one of his many concerns. Pompous bastard, he thought. It wasn't as if he was even the mayor or an elected official of the town; he just had a bigger wallet than anyone else. And so thinking he built a cigarette and poured a mug of Arbuckle's while he waited for the next do-gooder or busybody to pay a visit. He had smoked only half the quirly before the Reverend Jacob Mason came in. He was a stick-thin, perpetually nervous jasper with a curious nervous tic around his mouth that gave him a vaguely reptilian appearance.

'Bad business, Sheriff,' he said, entering and studiously avoiding eye-contact with the lawman. I've been to see the – er – doctor's woman, and she – er – she wants a quick burial. The boy – Vamoose he was called, I believe – has no kin, so I guess we can make a decision for him.' He stood, his hands fumbling with a small Bible that was ever present with him, and which he seemed to use like a set of worry beads.

The sheriff kept silent for a few moments longer than was necessary, since he enjoyed the padre's discomfort.

'Guess we can plant them as soon as possible then, Jacob.'

Still without looking in the sheriff's eyes, the Reverend Mason patted his pockets, transferred his Bible to his other hand and coughed.

'In that case I'll get Jud Farmery to get the coffins over to the doctor's place this morning. How would the funerals at two o'clock suit you?'

'Two is fine, Jacob.' And as he watched the padre scuttle away towards the town carpenter's work yard, he grinned. The sooner the better, he thought.

Burt Lister was a mass of pain. His arm hurt from the cauterized bullet wound, his head hurt from a humdinger of a hangover, but worst of all was the pain from his injured pride. He felt that the thing that would ease his pain most would be a result, something that would restore his name and get his reputation back up there where it belonged.

He was not in a mood for conversation as he walked along the back streets towards the sheriff's office.

'Señor Lister,' shouted the taller of two urchins who appeared from an alley.

He was about to wave them away as usual, but something in their manner made him stop and wait for them to run over to him. Their faces were both excited and fearful at the same time.

'We have something for you,' said the taller boy. 'We found it near where Vamoose was . . . killed.' He held out a small bundle with a trembling hand.

Lister took it and unwrapped the dirty cloth to reveal a bloodstained knife.

'Well, what do you know!' he whispered with satisfaction, no longer aware of any pain. 'Good work, *amigos*,' he said, beaming magnanimously. 'What say you show me exactly where you found this?' There was something puzzling about the knife, but he meant to solve the puzzle.

Just about the whole town turned out for the twin funeral of the town doctor, Sam Tolson, and of the local orphan, Vamoose, that afternoon. By any standards it was a swift funeral, conducted by the Reverend Mason according to Red Cloud's wishes, and Martha Cusworth's instructions, with minimal pious display. Throughout it all Red Cloud stood by the graveside, her face emotionless, not a single tear forming in her eyes; a complete contrast to the outpouring of emotion from the small group of urchins.

'Cold-blooded squaw!' someone murmured, setting off an undercurrent of unpleasantness.

Yet, if she heard anything, Red Cloud showed no sign of concern. She had loved Sam Tolson with a passion that she doubted whether anyone present could conceive of. No one perhaps except for Ethan and Abe, both of whom stood by her, admiring her fortitude and the pride that typified her people.

Slowly the crowd filed out of the cemetery, as Jud Farmery and his sons piled earth on top of the coffins. It was only when they too had patted the twin mounds and packed their tools away that she allowed any tears to come. Then she tossed her head back and cried once, before collapsing on top of the newly made grave of her man.

Both Abe and Ethan watched in horror as they saw her lie motionless on the earth, just as Laura Hollister had lain a few days previously.

Ethan and Abe took Red Cloud back and left her in Martha's care while they went to join the funeral wake which Abe had organized at the Dead Ringer. By the time they arrived, Nathaniel was run off his feet as the funeral throng stood three deep at the bar, everyone intent on wetting their whistles and drinking to the memory of the town doctor, if not to the memory of one of the town's orphans.

'I'll help Nathaniel,' Abe whispered, to Ethan. 'You just keep a low profile. Now ain't the time for music-making.'

So while Abe, Nathaniel and the other two barkeeps bustled about dispensing drinks behind the bar, Ethan found a seat at the end of the bar and poured himself a coffee from the ever-ready pot that stood there.

'Did you enjoy the funeral, *Zeke Kincaid*?' came a familiar voice from behind him.

Ethan turned to face the town sheriff.

'Are you loco, Sheriff? No one enjoys a funeral.'

Mat Hughes shook his head, his face impassive.

'I'm not loco, Zeke. But whoever killed the doc and that kid is loco. Maybe he would enjoy the funeral.'

Ethan stood up, conscious of the hush in the crowd and a shuffling of feet as people made room around him.

'I suggest you say what's really on your mind,

Sheriff. I don't like riddles.'

A slow smile formed on the lawman's face.

'I'm saying that I've got business with you, Zeke – or whatever your name really is – because people say they saw you leave last night with that kid, Vamoose. Then he turned up dead!'

Ethan felt a cold shiver run up his spine.

'I don't like what you're implying, Sheriff.'

Burt Lister's voice chipped in from the side.

'And Dirtville doesn't like murderers.'

Ethan saw the deputy out of the corner of his eye. He turned his head slowly.

'Murder is an ugly word, Lister!'

Burt Lister slowly and deliberately reached inside his vest and produced a small bundle.

'We found this where the kid was killed,' he announced, unwrapping the knife and holding it out for all to see. 'Nasty-looking thing, isn't it,' he said matter-of-factly. 'And look at the handle; it's got a couple of initials on it – E.G.'

Ethan felt his heart pound, but he willed himself to remain calm.

'My name is Zeke Kincaid. That's Z.K. not E.G.'

Mat Hughes gave an exaggerated nod.

'That's right! We had a guy with those initials come through here recently. Ethan Grant was his name, and he was wanted for two murders in Hagsworth.' He shook his head with mock sympathy. 'He's now a resident of Boot Hill.'

Abe Gibson raised his voice above the chorus of muttering that these words had prompted.

'Hey Sheriff, what are you getting at. Zeke had

nothing to do with these—'

'Shut up, Gibson,' snapped the sheriff. 'I'm not convinced that your piano-player is who he claims to be. And he still hasn't explained where he went with Vamoose. That's why I want his gun – now!'

Ethan felt beads of perspiration form on his brow. He cursed himself for allowing himself to get into such a position for the second time in as many days.

'I told you my name is Zeke Kincaid,' he said firmly, preparing himself for any sudden move from either the sheriff or the deputy.

He was unprepared for the man at the bar who had kept his back to him throughout all of the confrontation, and who now slowly turned round and grinned at him.

'Why hello, Ethan,' said Cole Burnett.

Despite himself, Ethan turned reflexively towards his former rival in love. Then the explosion of a gunshot registered in his brain at the same moment that he felt a bolt of pain in his side and he felt himself fall. As he looked up he saw the grinning face of Burt Lister towering over him, a smoking Remington .45 in his hand.

Then he passed out.

He awoke after a few moments to find countless faces peering down at him, then amid outraged cries of 'string him up' and 'hang the bastard' he heard a woman's voice cry out. He recognized the voice as Martha's. She was yelling to Abe and the sheriff.

'She's dead, Abe! Laura Hollister just died.'

He felt numerous hands dragging him up, manhandling him, but physical pain no longer meant anything to him. He hit out right and left, felt his fists connect with flesh and heard a few satisfying grunts of pain. Then someone slugged him on the back of the head and he felt himself diving into a pool of unconsciousness.

ELEVEN

Ethan clambered to consciousness and was immediately aware of seething pain in his head and in the left side of his chest. Upon opening his eyes he winced as if a thousand fiery needles had suddenly been pushed into his brain. He raised a hand to his head and felt a rag bandage that someone had bound round his crown. And as he moved, he felt another spasm in his side. Investigating, he found another crude bandage wrapped around his chest under his shirt.

Then he remembered the events in the Dead Ringer, and of how he had seen Cole Burnett's grinning face, and of how he had been shot by Burt Lister when he had turned to look at Burnett. And at the memory of Martha announcing that Laura had died he felt as if he had a gaping hole in the vicinity of his heart.

'Now we're even, Grant!'

Ethan painfully raised himself on his elbows and realized that he was lying on a bunk in the town jail. Three men were sitting looking at him from the office on the other side of the cell bars.

'You have to admit that was fancy shooting,' Lister said with a laugh. 'Couple of inches to the left and you'd be as dead as the other Ethan Grant we planted the other day.'

'You should have finished the job,' Ethan said.

'He didn't kill you, because that would have been cheating the law. Your killing spree has come to an end,' interjected the sheriff.

'I haven't killed anyone in my life,' Ethan said.

A third man dressed in a suit heaved himself to his feet and leaned on a cane.

'The court will decide that in due course, Grant. You don't know me, but I am Grover Wilkins, Walt Burnett's brother-in-law. If the court finds you guilty of his murder I'm going to watch you hang.'

Ethan swung his legs over the edge of the bunk and sat for a moment until a wave of dizziness passed. Then he stood and crossed to the cell door where he steadied himself against the bars.

'Mr Wilkins, I was going to come and see you. Cole Burnett gave me a letter to give you.'

The town entrepreneur sneered.

'And when were you going to give it to me? After you had your fun pretending to be someone else?'

'I was set up,' Ethan stated firmly, ignoring the sarcasm in Grover's voice. 'For some reason best known to himself Cole put a blank piece of paper in an envelope. I was bushwhacked when I came here by the Pintos trail. The jasper who did it robbed me and took my identity – to his mortal cost,' he added accusingly, as he glared at the deputy. 'Abe Gibson can back me up. Just ask him.'

Sheriff Hughes lit a quirly and blew out a thin stream of smoke.

'That's where you're wrong, mister. Abe Gibson says he wants nothing to do with you. He didn't like the way you held back about the kid, Vamoose. I reckon he's washed his hands of you.'

Ethan chewed his lip. He couldn't believe that Abe would abandon him like that.

The door opened and Cole Burnett came in.

'I'm just about ready, Uncle,' he said, nodding at Grover Wilkins. 'I've brought your horse and everything. Maybe you'd like to saddle up.'

Grover Wilkins tapped his cane reflectively on the floor.

'I'm ready, Cole. It'll be good to get away from Dirtville for a while. Its got a bad smell in it at the moment.' After nodding to the sheriff and his deputy he gave Ethan a final contemptuous glower, then left.

Cole Burnett turned his attention to Ethan and smiled malevolently.

'I sure am glad to see you've got this murdering crow behind bars, Sheriff Hughes.' He shook his head and tutted. 'But goodness me, Ethan, you look as if you've really fallen on hard times. All cut and bruised and wounded and all.' Again he smiled and added, 'And with a head bandage. Why you and the late Laura Hollister would have made a fine couple!'

Ethan saw red and shot a hand through the bars to grab Cole Burnett's throat. He squeezed and drew him nearer, his grip cutting the other's air supply and causing his face to go purple. The sheriff pistol-whipped Ethan's arm and the deputy hauled the gasping and coughing Cole Burnett away.

'I'll kill you, Cole!' Ethan gasped. 'So help me, I'll kill you.'

Cole Burnett eased himself upright and rubbed his throat.

'More death-threats, Ethan? Just how many folk do you need to kill to be happy. My father, Hank Turner, probably the Hagsworth telegrapher as well, and now Doc Tolson and a local street kid. Weren't they enough? Now you want to kill me as well?' He laughed sarcastically. 'I reckon you've got a big enough tally to warrant having your neck stretched before too long.'

Ethan rubbed his aching arm, all the time glaring at Burnett.

'I don't know what sort of game you're playing, Cole, but don't you ever say a word about Laura again, or I'll hunt you down – in this world or the next!'

Cole Burnett said nothing in reply. He backed to the door.

'Deputy Lister, it's been a pleasure knowing you. And Sheriff, I hope everything works out all right.'

Mat Hughes stubbed out his quirly.

'I'm sure it will, Mr Burnett,' he replied with a smile. 'It's all just the due process of law.'

Abe was nursing a whiskey and Martha Cusworth was sipping coffee in Doc Tolson's parlour when there was a forceful knock on the door. Before Martha could reach it, Red Cloud had appeared in the hall.

'Red Cloud, I thought I told you to rest,' said Martha.

'I must answer my husband's door,' she replied.

Burt Lister was standing on the threshold when she opened the door. She found his smile less than pleasant.

'What do you want?' Martha demanded over Red Cloud's shoulder.

'Law business,' Lister replied. 'The sheriff wants to follow up all leads. He needs to know for sure that the Hollister woman is dead.'

Red Cloud looked horrified and Martha gasped. She quickly regained her composure, as her temper flared.

'You monsters! Of course the poor thing is dead. How could you ask such a thing!'

'He said I've got to see her,' Lister persisted. 'What with there being no doctor to certify death, the sheriff needs to know for sure.' He raised his eyebrows at Red Cloud. 'So how about it, lady? Can you show me the body?'

Red Cloud's expressionless face belied the deep loathing that she felt for the town deputy. She stood barring his entrance.

'I don't see why the sheriff needs to send you!' Martha challenged.

'That's his affair,' Lister replied. 'Do you want me to go tell him that you're obstructing the law?'

Abe had come through on hearing the sound of confrontation.

'Actually Martha, I guess the deputy is right. Maybe you ought to let him see the body.'

Martha bit her lip then nodded. Putting her hand on Red Cloud's shoulder, she said:

'Let him in, dear. I'm sure that Sam would want you to do what the law asks.'

Red Cloud continued to stare at the deputy for a couple of moments, then, with a shrug of resignation stepped backwards and led the way through to the back room that they used for embalming.

Laura Hollister's body lay on the deal table, a sheet pulled over her head. Red Cloud pulled it back to reveal the still, motionless young woman whom she had cared for over the last few days. The complexion was alabaster-white and the lips a tinge of blue. The bandage was still bound around her head, a few stray tresses of corn-yellow hair hanging free. Red Cloud reached out and smoothed them back.

Burt Lister, despite all of his apparent bravado felt slightly nauseated at the sight, together with the heady smell of embalming fluid that hung in the air of the room. Although used to violent ends he felt strangely uneasy about this young woman's death. Guilt perhaps had etched its mark on his mind and, having confirmed the death, he wanted nothing more than to get out of this house of death and get some fresh air. To his mind the sooner she was buried the sooner he could forget that he had goaded her over the grave of the man they had all thought to be Ethan Grant.

'I'll tell the sheriff,' he said. 'I'm sure he'll be happy for you to get on with the burial as soon as you get her prepared.'

As he walked back to the office the nausea disappeared and once again he felt himself appreciating the doctor's widow. He grinned to himself.

'She just needs time,' he thought. 'Then maybe I'll call again.'

Sheriff Mat Hughes was also feeling pretty good about things. Cole Burnett had taken Grover Wilkins off his hands and the townsfolk seemed to be settling down, now that he had the murderer under lock and key. After Burt Lister had returned with the confirmation of the Hollister girl's death he had sent the deputy away for a bite of dinner while he sat and smoked a cigar.

'I guess I ought to offer you a cigar,' he said through the bars to Ethan. 'A condemned man is entitled to a last request.'

'Ain't you forgetting something, Sheriff,' Ethan replied. 'I haven't even been tried, let alone condemned.'

'Matter of time, mister. The evidence is all there. I reckon you'll hang within the week.' He grinned. 'Anyway, I'm afraid this is my last cigar.' He continued smoking and Ethan lay down on his bunk and closed his eyes. His situation was desperate, there was no mistaking, but he was not the type to roll over and accept his fate. He felt miserable in the knowledge that Laura had died, which made his wrongful imprisonment impossible to bear. He had been stitched up by Cole Burnett, of that he had no doubt, just as he had no doubt now that the rancher's son had intended to land him in trouble from the very first when he sent him to Dirtville with a blank piece of paper in an envelope. He had always suspected that he was worthless, yet he found it hard to believe that he could be responsible for the murder of his own father.

And as he lay there feigning sleep his anger festered. He had to get out to find Cole and get the truth out of him. And he needed to get out to deal with that mongrel of a deputy whom he believed to be responsible for Laura's death, albeit indirectly. He was just imagining what he'd do to Lister when the said person walked into the office.

'Has he been giving you any trouble, Sheriff?'

Mat Hughes blew a smoke ring and smiled contentedly.

'Not a bit, Burt. We had a chat about his future, or lack of one, and he's gone off to sleep like a babe.' He chortled and puffed again on his cigar stub.

'Do you want to go eat now?' Lister asked.

'Soon.' Hughes put his feet on the edge of the desk and pointed at Ethan with his cigar. 'He was fast with a gun, wasn't he? Pity you'll never know if you could have taken him.'

The deputy sniffed. 'I'd have whipped him. You saw what I did earlier. I could have dropped him, but I even had enough time to just graze him.'

Ethan opened his eyes. 'Brave talk when you can never prove it,' he said.

'I had you dead, mister!'

'You shot when you knew I wasn't looking,' replied Ethan. 'It was a sandbagging that you arranged with that dog Burnett – a cowardly bushwhacking, just like

138

that time you shot that other guy in the back of the head.' He sat up. 'Only a coward shoots from behind!'

Burt Lister's face went puce.

'Don't ever call me a coward, pilgrim. I could take you any time.'

'Yeah? Then let's do it!' Ethan challenged. He stood up and gripped the bars of the cell. 'Of course, I have no gun, which is just as well for you.'

'Easy, Burt,' said Hughes, sensing that Ethan's goading was hitting home with his deputy. He stood and dropped his cigar butt in the ashtray. 'Don't let him rile you.'

'Let's do it, Sheriff,' Lister said. 'Give him a gun and I'll show him. It'll save the town the cost of a rope.' He took a step forward. 'I'm ready for you any time, mister.'

'Yes, Sheriff, do it,' Ethan replied, feeling his raw anger rising. At that moment the thing he wanted more than anything else in the world was to face the deputy with a gun at his side. To avenge Laura's death.

The two men faced each other, hatred in their eyes, neither wanting the sheriff to intervene.

The sheriff said nothing for a moment, as if he was considering the matter seriously. Then:

'Are you sure about this, Burt?'

Lister nodded. 'Give him a gun and let's do it now.'

'I don't know, Burt,' said Hughes. 'This isn't right.' He took a step forward until he was a mere pace behind his deputy. 'But if you insist . . .'

Ethan was oblivious to all except the deputy's eyes. He wanted to face him man to man. He did not expect to see the sheriff's hand snake round and grasp the deputy's forehead and pull it backwards; to see the knife appear from the other side and slash across the exposed throat, severing carotid arteries and windpipe. An arc of spurting blood showered him and he flinched and stepped backwards, looking horrified as the deputy's hands went futilely to his gaping throat, and his body convulsed before pitching forward to lie lifeless on the floor.

'You shouldn't have insisted, Burt,' said the sheriff, shaking his head with a sadistic smile. He drew his gun and pointed it at Ethan.

'Not a sound!' he said.

Cole Burnett led the way along the Pintos canyon trail. They had started off in the blistering heat, but as the long shadows of the canyon walls shaded them from the sun the temperature dropped considerably.

Grover Wilkins puffed contentedly on his pipe as he rode along. 'This has been a bad business, Cole,' he said at length. 'I must say I'm pleased to see Ethan Grant behind bars.'

Cole looked over his shoulder and smiled wanly.

'Not that it will bring my pa back, but I agree, the bastard deserves to hang. I reckon we should be back in time to see him swing.'

Grover tapped his teeth with the mouthpiece of his pipe.

'I still find it strange, though.'

Cole stopped and waited for his uncle to draw alongside.

'What's strange, Uncle Grover.'

'Why, just that Walt never seemed . . .' Then his eyes opened wide in alarm as he looked at his nephew and found himself staring into the barrel of a Colt .45. His pipe fell from his mouth. 'What the hell!'

Cole laughed. 'Surprise, surprise, eh, Uncle?' The gun swiftly rose and fell, hammering down on Grover's head. He tumbled sideways off his horse to land in the dirt, blood flowing freely down the side of his face from the gash on his head. 'And that is the first of my pay-backs.'

The Dirtville entrepreneur sat up painfully.

'What are you talking about, boy?'

'I hated it when you called me that when I was a kid,' said Cole. 'Especially after one of your beatings.' He grinned maliciously. 'But I really do hate it now, so here's pay-back number two.'

Grover stared in horror as his nephew took careful aim, then shot him in his good leg.

TWELVE

Ethan watched in stunned disbelief as the sheriff casually locked the office door and lit the oil-lamp on his desk. Then he grabbed his dead deputy's collar and dragged his body across the office to the foot of the cell door. He gestured with his gun and Ethan moved backwards.

'He was a good deputy,' Hughes said matter-of-factly, as he put a toe under the torso and heaved the corpse over, so that Lister's face was staring straight up at the ceiling and the ugly gaping wound continued to ooze and contribute to the expanding pool of blood. 'But he still has his uses.'

'You're mad!' gasped Ethan.

Sheriff Hughes laughed, but it was not the laugh of a madman, rather that of one who is rather pleased at his own cleverness. He picked up the knife, which he had placed on the desk, and hefted it in his hand. 'I knew it would have more use in it,' he said. 'Cole said it was a first-rate killing knife, and he was right.' He let it drop beside Lister's body.

'Are you saying that Burnett killed Doc Tolson and Vamoose?'

The sheriff drew out the cell key and opened the door, all the while keeping his Colt trained on the centre of Ethan's chest.

'Both of them. And now you and me are going on a little trip. But first things first, turn around real slow.'

Ethan did as he was told, half-expecting instant death. Instead he felt handcuffs being clasped shut on his wrists. Then he was dragged out of the cell and pushed in the direction of the rear door.

'We'll have time for a good ride and a chinwag at the other end,' said the sheriff. 'I expect a posse should be following in a few hours.'

Grover Wilkins writhed in agony as he tried to stanch the flow of blood from the wound in his calf.

'You dog!' he spat. 'What the hell has gotten into you, Cole?'

Cole Burnett had dismounted and tied both horses to a spindly scrub-oak.

'Revenge, Uncle,' he replied, squatting in front of him. 'You were a bastard to me and my ma all the time my pa was away at the War. You beat me sometimes when you had no reason to.'

'Reckon I didn't beat you enough.'

Cole grinned. 'And then you always kept Pa on a string. Always wanted your share of his profits.'

'Well, it was my ranch,' Grover replied indignantly. 'Walt was competent, but no more than that. At least I let him pretend to everyone that it was his ranch. It was the least I could do in memory of my little sister, your ma.'

Cole Burnett laughed. 'And do you realize something, Uncle. Now there's just you and me.'

'So that's it! You want the ranch, the mine and everything else.'

Cole Burnett went to his saddle-bag, drew out a sheaf of papers and unfastened his canteen from around the horn.

'Wash your hands, Uncle,' he said, tossing the canteen into his uncle's lap. 'I don't want any blood-stains showing when you write your will.'

Ethan rode Lister's horse with his knees, since his hands were cuffed behind him. Making a break for it was out of the question, for he was all too aware of Sheriff Hughes riding behind him with his gun at the ready. And the bandanna that he had been gagged with removed any chance of alerting anyone. Not that there was anyone to alert. They had left the jail by the back way and ridden through the back streets to take the trail towards Pintos Canyon. Once they had crossed the semi-desert bedecked with saguaro cacti and patches of scrub-oak, Mat Hughes became talkative. A slight slur in his voice made Ethan realize that the occasional sloshing noises than he had heard behind him had been due to the sound of a bottle being drunk from.

'Guess it's all a mystery to you, Ethan Grant,' Hughes said sarcastically. 'One day all's well, you've just got your cows to look after, and then – bang! bang! Your world has fallen apart and you're a wanted man.' The sheriff laughed and they rode on into the canyon, the light rapidly failing. 'Don't you worry none about losing the way. Lister's horse is a clever beast; he won't let you get lost. And soon you'll learn everything. We just gotta go up the trail a couple of miles, then you can have a rest.' He drank more from the bottle and laughed heartily. 'A good long rest!'

Grover leaned back against a rock and ground his teeth to try to distract himself from the pain that was racking his body. At first he had refused to follow his nephew's dictation, until Cole had put another bullet into his foot.

'Each time you refuse you'll forfeit a toe,' he had said with an evil leer. 'Now you've only got four left.'

The pain was excruciating, but Grover could see no escape, no way of turning the tables. His nephew was clearly a cold-blooded bloodsucker who was probably going to kill him anyway. Only by doing exactly as he was told did he have any chance of survival. But he wondered how long he'd be able to hold on, for apart from the pain from his wounds, he was steadily losing blood.

At last Cole took the paper from him and began to read:

' "*Last Will and Testament of Grover Wilkins, made this 17th day of March 1885.*" ' He grinned. 'That's good, Uncle, very good. It'll look as if you made it a couple of months back. And of course, you've left everything that you own to your next of kin, your ever-loving nephew, Cole Burnett. Now I'm going to be real good to you and fix up some coffee.'

And while he prepared a camp-fire and got a pot of Arbuckles on the brew, he smoked a cigar. He was still smoking it when they heard the sound of approaching horses.

'Well, lookee here,' Cole said, pointing to the two horsemen advancing out of the shadows. 'Maybe you're going to be rescued, Uncle. I do believe it's the Dirtville Sheriff!' And he put two fingers to his mouth and gave a shrill whistle. It was immediately answered and a few moments later the horsemen entered the ring of camp-fire light.

'Howdy Cole, howdy Grover,' said the sheriff. 'I brought another friend to join our little party.' And reaching forward he shoved Ethan, who was unable to check himself. He fell winded on the ground beside Grover.

'Did it all go as planned?' Cole Burnett asked.

'Like a dream,' Sheriff Hughes replied.

Grover Wilkins had looked in shocked amazement, first at the Dirtville sheriff, then at the manacled and gagged Ethan Grant, who was struggling to sit upright.

'Don't tell me that you're in on this too, Mat?'

Burnett and the sheriff looked at each other and grinned.

'We're partners,' Hughes replied. 'And soon we're gonna be damned rich partners.' He produced his bottle and took a swig of whiskey. 'Me, I fancy being a gentleman rancher, instead of a dogsbody lawman.'

Ethan managed to push himself back against the same rock that Grover was leaning against. He nodded his head and Grover reached up and pulled his gag free. Ethan worked his jaw muscles and worked up some saliva.

'These two have been on a murdering spree,' he said. 'Cole there murdered Doc Tolson and that poor kid, Vamoose. Then that sheriff cut his deputy's throat in front of my own eyes.'

The sheriff snorted with whiskey-soaked glee.

'But who would believe any of that? No one! But they will believe that you did it, because of course as far as everyone in town is aware, you're in jail for two of those murders this minute.'

Cole Burnett sneered at his former rival.

'And when they find the deputy, they'll add two and two together.' He handed the will to the sheriff. 'All you got to do now, Mat, is sign my uncle's will and then we start to get rich.'

The lawman squatted down by the fire and signed his name, also dating it two months previously. He handed it back to Burnett and rose. He wiped the mouth of the bottle with his palm and held it out. 'What say we have a little toast, Cole?'

The gun blast caught him full in the chest and he fell back across the fire, blood spurting from a chest wound. His hand clawed reflexively towards his own gun, but was halted as a second shot through the heart sent him to hell.

'Two's too many,' Cole Burnett explained. 'And now I'm afraid that I'm going to have to leave you, too. Goodbye Uncle!'

Grover raised his arms as if to fend off a bullet, but to no avail. Cole Burnett shot him in the chest. He laughed as the body fell sideways against Ethan.

'You bastard! You murdering bastard!' Ethan began, tensing himself for the fatal shot.

But it did not come. Instead, Cole Burnett struck a light to his cigar and stood casually, smoking.

'Don't worry, Ethan. I'm not going to kill you.' He sniggered as he replaced his uncle's forged will in his saddlebag. 'I'm not going to have to,' he explained. 'I reckon the posse may do that themselves.' He looked up at the sturdy looking scrub-oak that stood a few paces away. 'That looks like a good hanging-tree.'

He advanced towards Ethan and raised his Colt. He brought it viciously down on Ethan's head and grinned to himself as Ethan slumped sideways. Then he turned to the sheriff's corpse and fished in his pockets for the key of the handcuffs.

'It'll be quite a sight for the posse,' he said to himself. 'I reckon that you might just wake in time to make a break for it. Otherwise, Ethan, you're a dead man.'

Cole Burnett prided himself on being a careful man. As he picked a circuitous route back through the Pintos, he gave himself a mental pat on the back. He had heard the posse coming along the main trail, as he suspected he would, and saw in the moonlight that it was made up of about five men.

'Planned to perfection,' he whispered gloatingly, as he watched them from his concealment behind a huge red boulder. 'You'll get to Ethan just in time to hang him before you turn in for the night, then you'll get back to Dirtville in time for breakfast!' He laughed softly as he watched them make their way along. 'And this is going to give me all the time I need.'

The rest of his ride was uneventful all the way to Dirtville. He dismounted and walked his horse through the back alleys and let himself into Grover Wilkins' house with the key that he found in the old man's vest pocket. He made his way straight to the study and in a matter of moments planted the will among his uncle's legal documents.

'Reckon I deserve a drink,' he muttered, spying the decanter on the desk. He poured three fingers of rye and sat back in Grover's comfortable leather armchair. He put his feet up on the desk.

Plenty of time, he thought, relishing the feeling of the rye as it hit his stomach. Minutes later, he had fallen asleep.

Zach Holmes and Judge Arthur Hollister had left Hagsworth after the rider from Sheriff Hughes gave them the message about Laura being the mystery woman lying in a coma in Dirtville. Zach had already repaired the line, which had been effectively sabotaged in several locations, but had been prevented from telegraphing to Dirtville on account of his being the only trained telegrapher in town. Upon hearing of Willard Cox's murder he had drunk half a bottle of whiskey and let off a dozen rounds of ammunition into an innocent saguaro cactus, cussing with each shot and wishing that he had his friend and colleague's murderer in his sights.

Understandably, Judge Hollister was in a state of

high anxiety, which accounted for them hiring Clem Chambers to drive a special Concord through the night on the trail round the Pintos. They were both at a point of almost total exhaustion by the time they arrived in Dirtville, soon after daybreak.

They went straight to the sheriff's office, where they were greeted by the sight of a couple of heavily armed Dirtville citizens dozing in chairs beside the locked door. After rousing the men, Zach cajoled them into giving a graphic account of the events of the past few days, culminating in the murder of the deputy, Burt Lister.

'The posse's gone after Ethan Grant,' said one of the men, a portly bar-dog from one of the town's drinking-houses. 'And it looks as if the sheriff had already gone after the bastard, after he found Lister in there with his throat cut from ear to ear.'

The other man prodded his compatriot and nodded in the judge's direction.

'My God!' exclaimed the first, realizing the glaring omission in his account. 'The Hollister girl! She – she's—'

Judge Hollister grabbed him by his vest lapels.

'She's what?' he demanded, his eyes wide in alarm.

'Dead!' said the other man, gulping as soon as the words came out.

Judge Hollister stared at him in disbelief for a moment, then abruptly he staggered and was helped into a chair by Zach, who glared angrily at Ned Palmer, the unwitting messenger of this tragedy.

The sound of a galloping horse broke the silence that had fallen and a moment later Cole Burnett rounded a corner and charged up the street towards them. He hauled on his reins, bringing his horse to a halt by the hitching-rail.

'Judge! Thank God! I've got to get Deputy Lister. Ethan Grant attacked us – my uncle and me – in Pintos canyon. He – he shot my uncle, then Sheriff Hughes rode in to help – and Grant shot him as well! The deputy has gotta get a posse up real quick.'

'Deputy Lister is dead!' announced Zach.

Cole Burnett looked horrified. 'Lister is dead? How?'

'Throat cut,' returned Ned Palmer, making a slicing gesture across his own throat. 'Grant must have had a concealed knife on him when they arrested him, and he waited until he had a chance to grab Lister from behind. Then he escaped.'

'Well, let's get some men together ourselves,' Cole Burnett said. 'I've been riding all night and I'm tired, but I can lead the way.'

A crowd had rapidly begun to congregate, some in early-morning work clothes, others in night attire, all attracted by the commotion outside the jail. From the crowd a boy's voice called out:

'He is lying, *señors*! He has been in Señor Grover Wilkins' house for the past three hours.'

Cole Burnett's eyes spied the group of street urchins, and rested on the tallest one, seemingly Vamoose's successor.

'Shut up, you damned whelp!' he cried.

The boy cowered slightly, but held his ground.

'I saw him, *señor*,' he went on. 'We saw him sneak into town and go to Señor Wilkins' house. He has

151

been in there drinking whiskey.'

Cole Burnett was about to shout again, when a cacophony of noise came from the other end of the town, followed a few moments later by the appearance of the posse. There were five riders leading two horses on which bodies were bent forward across the horses' necks, their arms hanging either side.

One of the riders detached himself from the group and rode forward.

'We got him!' cried Dan Bannion. 'We got the murdering bastard.'

And as the group came up the street it was apparent that one of the men had his hands bound. Ethan Grant had clearly taken a beating. One eye was closed and his jaw was swollen and his nose was bloodied.

'You got the swine, by God!' exclaimed Cole Burnett, edging his horse backwards. 'He almost did for me too.'

At the sound of Burnett's voice Ethan raised his head.

'You lying cur, Burnett. I'll—'

He was silenced by a slap across the face from Beanie, the lanky member of the trio that Ethan had bested in the Dead Ringer. He was about to strike again, but was himself halted by Nathaniel Grogan, one of the posse.

'Don't touch him again, Beanie Driscoll, or I'll give you a taste of your own medicine.' He looked at the judge. 'I had the devil of a job stopping these coyotes from lynching this prisoner.'

Todd Reardon and his two associates started cursing and complaining, but were stopped by Judge Hollister's authoritative voice.

'Shut your mouths! This town is under my jurisdiction and every man is entitled to a fair trial – even someone like Ethan Grant.'

Ethan turned his head so that he could see the judge with his good eye. He shook his head sorrowfully.

'Laura! Have – have you heard?'

The judge hung his head. 'I've heard.'

'Dammit! This dog doesn't deserve a trial!' cried Cole Burnett. 'He killed my pa and Hank Turner. Now he's killed the Dirtville sheriff and his deputy. Are we going to let him get away with that?'

There were murmurings of agreement from the crowd. Then Abe Gibson pushed his way to the front.

'That's a lie, mister, and you know it,' he cried. 'Ethan hasn't killed anyone.'

Cole Burnett felt a trickle of cold perspiration run down his back.

'What are you talking about? He killed your sheriff and that dirty kid.'

A woman's voice, quavering a little called out:

'You're a liar and a murderer, Cole Burnett!'

Burnett's face went as pale as death and he stared aghast as the crowd parted to reveal three women. Red Cloud and Martha were supporting Laura Hollister between them. Her head was still bandaged and she looked ashen and weak, yet there was undoubted determination in her manner.

'I saw you, Cole. I saw you murder Walt Burnett, your own father. Then you shot Hank Turner. Walt had gone out to confront you after he found out about how you had salted that mine of yours with gold nuggets you had bought. He found a receipt.'

'Laura! You're alive! Thank God,' gasped Judge Hollister. Then he darted a glance at Cole Burnett and raised a finger at him. 'Get down off that horse.'

But Burnett's hand had dived inside his vest and come out with a knife. He raised it behind his head.

'Damn you, Laura!' He flung the knife at her.

Red Cloud had looked after Laura Hollister so intensely that she immediately turned and threw herself forward to protect her patient. They fell backwards, dragging Martha with them, and the knife sailed over them to embed itself in the doorframe of the saddler's shop.

Burnett kicked the sides of his horse and fled, as everyone, including the armed posse members, stared in horror at the sight of the three women on the ground and the knife quivering in the wood above them. Ethan was the first to react. He kicked the flanks of Burt Lister's horse and charged off in hot pursuit.

Seeing Ethan making a break for it prompted Todd Reardon to unholster and raise his weapon to aim at Ethan's back. But Nathaniel knocked his hand aside and the bullet went wide.

Ethan overtook Burnett's horse by the outskirts of town. He heaved himself out of the saddle to take Burnett with him in a rolling dive. Both winded, they rose together, Burnett with fists flaying.

'I'm going to kill you, Grant. You should be dead already, damn you!'

But Ethan ducked the blows and coming up with bound fists delivered a double-handed haymaker that lifted his rival off his feet and deposited him, stuporous, on his back. Then Ethan was on him, his hands seizing his throat and squeezing frenziedly.

Then he felt Abe Gibson's hand on his shoulder.

'No, Ethan!' he said. 'He's finished his double-dealing. Don't let him cheat the rope.'

EPILOGUE

The trial of Cole Burnett was held a week later, by which time Laura Hollister had recovered considerably.

As had Grover Wilkins.

The local businessman was all too aware that he had stared death in the face and somehow been spared. His chest wound had resulted in a punctured lung and the loss of a considerable amount of blood, yet he was blessed with a tough, stubborn streak and he was determined to face his would-be murderer in court. He sat in the courtroom in a dilapidated bath chair, his chest bandaged and skilfully dressed by Red Cloud, and listened as Laura Hollister gave her account.

'He murdered Walt Burnett and Hank Turner in cold blood,' she concluded. 'I knew that Ethan would be in danger, so I rode back to Hagsworth and caught the first stage to Dirtville.'

She told of how Burt Lister had cruelly shown her the grave that bore the name of Ethan Grant. 'Then my mind just snapped,' she said. 'I . . . I felt that I had nothing to live for.'

Judge Hollister had clearly found it difficult to have to hear his daughter's testimony, but he did a professional job. He dismissed her, then called Abe Gibson to the stand. Abe explained how he and Zach Holmes had witnessed Laura's confrontation with the town deputy, and of how they had seen her shoot herself and fall over the grave. Then he explained about going off into the Pintos Canyon and finding Ethan, and of how they between them manufactured the character of Zeke Kincaid, so that Ethan could find out what was happening in Dirtville.

Gradually, the picture was painted of the plan cooked up by the sheriff and Cole Burnett to fleece Grover Wilkins out of his money, by getting him to invest in a worthless mine. Through all of this Cole Burnett sat, apparently disinterested and unconcerned. It was only when Ethan took his place in the witness box that he registered any emotion. That emotion was blind hatred.

'You're a lying dog!' he screamed, as Ethan gave his account of being sent to Dirtville with a couple of bags of gold-dust and an empty envelope. 'You killed my pa! You poisoned him!' he yelled. 'You poisoned him against me.'

'Silence in court!' boomed Judge Hollister, rapping his gavel on the table.

But Cole Burnett paid no attention, and continued to rant.

'Ethan this, Ethan that! The old fool was besotted with you, instead of with me, his only son! That's why I sent you here – to disgrace yourself in his eyes.'

The judge rapped his gavel again.

'I'll tell you when to talk, Cole Burnett. Now keep quiet.'

But Burnett seemed to have eyes for no one but Ethan.

'Then that fool ambushed you and got himself killed by the deputy, I saw a way of getting rid of you once and for all. And a way of getting what should be mine by rights.' He glared at Grover Wilkins, then he tossed his head back and laughed; the laugh of a man on the very edge of sanity. 'And you have left me everything, haven't you Uncle Grover? This whole town is just about mine now, you left it to me in your will.' And then the laughter became positively maniacal.

Judge Hollister had little option but to adjourn the trial. He signalled for Zach Holmes and Nathaniel Grogan, the acting Dirtville deputies, to take Burnett away.

Abe Gibson nudged Martha, who was sitting beside him.

'He's mad, or a good pretender,' he whispered.

'He's more than mad,' Martha replied. 'He's mad and bad, and I hope that he rots in hell after all that he's done.'

The trial was restarted a week later, after a doctor had been drafted in to examine Cole Burnett and pronounce him to be perfectly sane. Following that there was little doubt about the outcome, especially when Grover Wilkins gave his testimony and produced the will that he had been made to write under duress, and which also bore Sheriff Mat Hughes' guilty signature. Judge Henry Hollister passed the death sentence on him, and had him dragged away, screaming obscenities.

The whole of Dirtville was full of the news and the gossipmongers spread the story wide, to the passing-through Concord passengers, to outlying farms and ranches. The fact that the Dirtville sheriff had been in cahoots with Cole Burnett, and that he had murdered his own deputy, made everyone suspicious of appointing another sheriff. Until Nathaniel Grogan, whom everyone knew, decided to give up drink-dispensing and pin on the star. He was a man they felt they could trust.

'It's all been a nightmare, Ethan,' Laura said a few evenings later, as they stood in the moonlit porch outside Grover Wilkins' house. 'I can't believe that Cole had so much hate in him, so much wickedness.'

Ethan nodded and folded her in his arms.

'He was greedy and evil, Laura. He wanted Grover's money, at first just by cooking up that scheme with the sheriff. Then after he killed Walt, I figure he just lost his mind and set out on killing anyone who got in his way. And that included Sam Tolson and that boy, Vamoose. Now, he's going to pay the ultimate penalty for all his double-dealing.'

'So we can get on with our lives, Ethan? Can we...?'

'Get married? Sure thing, as long as you can cope with being a rancher's wife.'

Laura stared quizzically at him.

Ethan grinned and reached inside his vest and

drew out a folded bill.

'That's right, honey, a rancher. Mr Wilkins signed over the Rocking WB to me this afternoon. It's all signed, sealed and approved by the judge.'

The door had been opened without their realizing and Grover Wilkins' voice cut in.

'It's a wedding gift,' he said. He was sitting in the bath chair, pushed by Red Cloud. 'I kinda think that Walt would have been happy knowing that Ethan was going to look after the spread. And after all you two have been through, it's the least I can do to make amends.'

' 'Course, you two have got to get married first,' said Abe Gibson over Grover's shoulder. His arm was around Martha Cusworth's waist. 'And if you want, well, Martha and I would be proud if we could make it a double wedding day.'

Judge Hollister appeared from inside with a glass of whiskey in his hand.

'I think I'll drink to that, so long as I get to do the marrying.'

Ethan and Laura looked at each other, then laughed.

'Now that sounds an altogether better kind of double-deal for Dirtville. What do you say, honey?'

Laura drew his head towards her waiting lips.

'Do you really need to ask, Ethan!'